CUBICLE WARFARE

CUBICLE WARFARE

101 OFFICE TRAPS AND PRANKS

John Austin

Collins
An Imprint of HarperCollinsPublishers

HarperCollins books may be purchased for educational, business, or sales promotional use. For information please write: Special Markets Department, HarperCollins Publishers, 10 East 53rd Street, New York, NY 10022.

FIRST EDITION

This book is written as a source of information containing only the highest quality of pranks. All efforts have been made to ensure the effectiveness of our pranks and the accuracy of the information contained in this book as of the date published. The author and the publisher expressly disclaim responsibility for any adverse effects arising from the use or application of the information contained herein, including the termination of your job, the loss of your friends, or the angry looks you'll get from coworkers.

Designed by Reshma Chattaram

Library of Congress Cataloging-in-Publication Data

Austin, John, 1978–
  Cubicle warfare : 101 office traps and pranks / John Austin.—1st ed.
    p. cm.
  ISBN 978-0-06-143886-8
  1. Humor in the workplace. 2. Offices—Humor. 3. Practical jokes. 4. Tricks.
I. Title.

  HF5549.5.H85A97 2008
  650.1'3—dc22

                                                                 2007044299

08 09 10 11 12 ID3/RRD 10 9 8 7 6 5 4 3 2 1

ACKNOWLEDGEMENTS

The author would like to thank all the extremely talented designers at the Bro: Archer, Bono, Boudreaux, Mr. Boyce, Mr. Chapman, DK, Dube, Eddins, Fardie, Farrah, Mr. Foster, Grimes, Rob Harper, Hayes, The Jinks, Mr. Johnson, Judkins, Mr. Lamb Lewinski, Marcus, Steve Masso, Mead, Mckamy, Panzica, Paolino, Wayne Park, Parrish, Rawley, Steve Redinger, Paul Pouliot, Sass, Siebenaler, Mr. Stall, Vikie Stratford, Vonner, Wade, Warden, Mr. Wilk, Mr. Wise, Ham Woodhouse, and of course, Lynn Janke and Linda Lianos, as well as Kirk Bauer, Steve Mayo, Frank Sterpka, Dead Monkeys, Laurie Abkemeier, Matthew Benjamin, Reshma Chattaram, Anne Cole, Lorie Pagnozzi, and the entire team at HarperCollins!

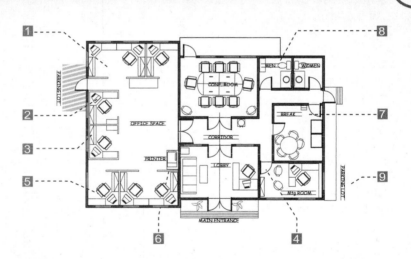

1 Cubicle Space
2 Desktop Disasters
3 Office Cabinets
4 Office Entrance
5 Computer Abuse

6 Electronic Equipment
7 Break Time
8 Lavatory
9 Parking Lot

CONTENTS

Introduction   xiii

CONTENTS (CONT'D)

INTRODUCTION

Cubicle Warfare is your training guide to the top weapons and strategies for transforming yourself from a cube monkey into a corporate commando. This is your fully illustrated manual to more than 100 beautifully designed pranks and cunning traps. This book is the ammo you need in the fight against the suits and the squares.

It's time to fight back!

CUBICLE SPACE

DIFFICULTY LEVEL 1

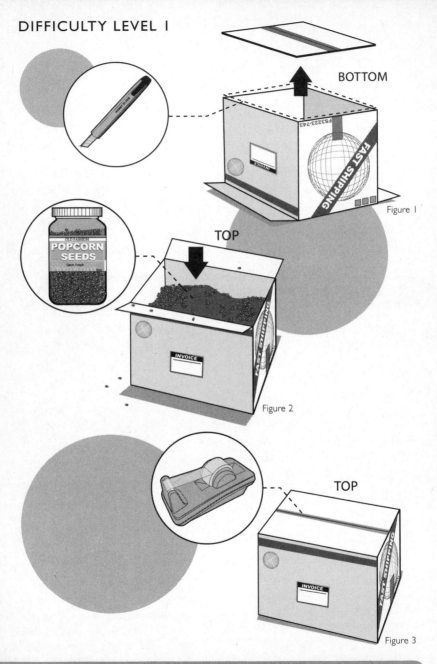

BOTTOM

Figure 1

TOP

Figure 2

TOP

Figure 3

Figure 4

1) Remove the bottom of a random shipping box.
Use a utility knife to create a clean cut around the bottom of the box (Figure 1).

2) Place the box in front of your coworker's office.
Set down the box in the middle of your mark's door, so he or she will be tempted to pick it up. Next, fill the box up with thousands of popcorn seeds (Figure 2). Remember not to pick up the box after this step, because you removed the bottom . . . remember?

3) Seal the top of the parcel with industrial packing tape.
Use parcel tape to seal the lid of the box. Not only does this add to its authenticity of a real parcel, but it also entices your mark to carry it to his desk to open it (Figure 3).

4) Wait quietly for your coworker to return.
As soon as your victim picks up the tainted box, thousands of popcorn seeds pour out onto the floor (Figure 4).

Who deserves this? That guy who gets the most packages.

SEE ME

DIFFICULTY LEVEL I

Figure 1

Figure 2

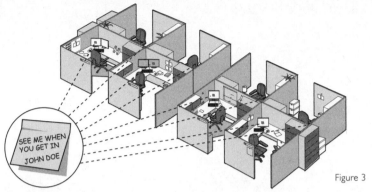

Figure 3

1) Carry out this mission late one night!

This simple but very effective corporate antic concentrates on the pure fundamentals of psychological office warfare. The ideal time of execution is late one night when you find yourself surrounded by only custodial staff.

2) Fill out a ton of sticky notes.

Armed with only your penmanship and a handful of sticky notes, begin to fill duplicate notes with the saying "See me when you get in." Then sign your mark's signature (Figure 1).

3) Walk around the office and place the "See Me" notes on everyone's monitor.

Start with everyone who knows your victim first, and then place the excess on random monitors around the office (Figure 2).

4) Come in early the next morning to witness the interruptions.

Unbeknownst to your victim, he or she will settle into the daily morning routine. Then it starts. Little by little, employees trickle into their individual offices, read the note, and then venture down to your mark's office. The more notes, the bigger the payoff (Figure 3).

 Who deserves this? The VP with eyes on the corner office.

DIFFICULTY LEVEL 1

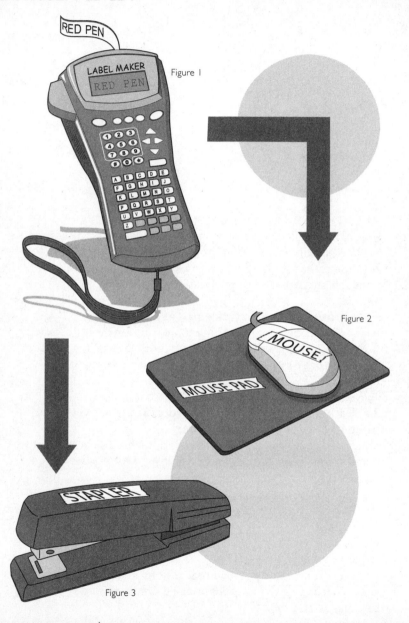

Figure 1

Figure 2

Figure 3

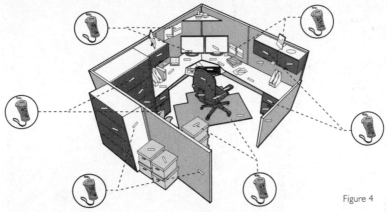

Figure 4

1) Lock and load!

It is fairly simple; just break out the label maker and hit everything in your victim's office—from the storage boxes, cabinets, shelves, and folders to pens, pencils, keyboard, mouse, monitor, chair, paper clip, phone, phone cord, speakers, headphones, plants, pictures, people in the pictures, radio, and of course the coffee mug (Figures 1–4).

2) Team up with a fellow coworker to increase your labeling effort!

It is probably best to team up on this one, or be prepared for some strange carpal tunnel issues from all the micro typing!

Who deserves this? Anyone with obsessive-compulsive behavior who could use a lavish label makeover.

DIFFICULTY LEVEL I

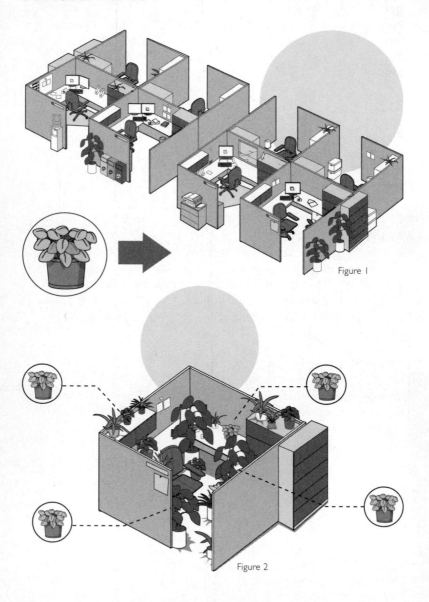

Figure 1

Figure 2

1) Gather up all the vegetation you can get your green thumbs on.

Notice an abundance of plants in your area? During non-work hours, gather up all the plants in the office (Figure 1). You may want to use a small presentation cart to truck the load to the plants' new destination.

2) Relocate the borrowed plants to your victim's space.

Plastic or real, fill up the space (Figure 2). I can guarantee you this overgrown mess will upset more than one person. It might be a good idea to label each plant with possible extensions or office numbers.

➡ Who deserves this? That VP who infested the entire floor with bugs from his exotic plants.

(!) Another suggestion:

You can purchase fake marijuana plants on the Internet. Place this Mary Jane in the lobby by all the other plants (Figure 3). It will be interesting to see who notices it first.

! Fake Marijuana Plant

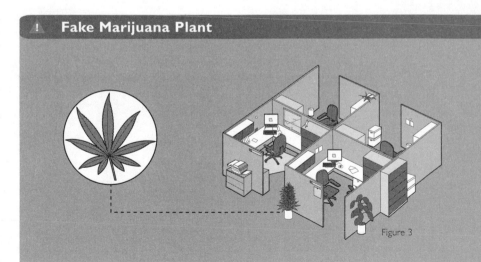

Figure 3

DIFFICULTY LEVEL 1

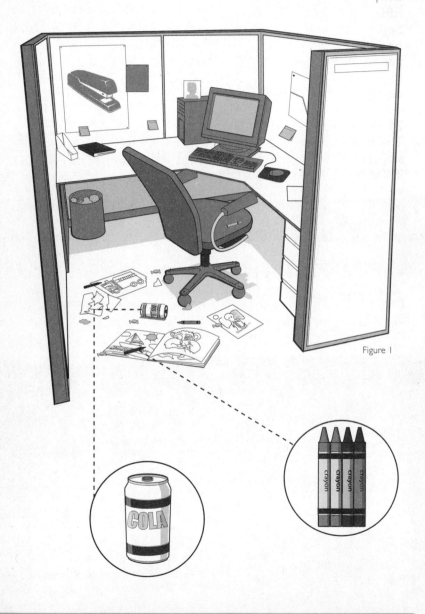

Figure 1

1) Nothing like escaping from your chaotic home only to come to work and find a huge mess made by kids in your office.

Set up your associate's office as if some random kid had been playing in it for hours during the previous night. Candy wrappers, coloring books, empty pop cans, and a few toys are a total giveaway. Place all the props on the floor in a childish disarray (Figure 1).

2) Once she sees it, expect a few expletives.

The first reaction will be priceless. It will start with confusion, then cursing, and then a bombardment of questions. If she asks you, reply with "I think the boss had his kids in yesterday." Periodically execute this over the course of a month.

➡ **Who deserves this?** The mother who just returned from leave and won't stop talking about her kids.

(!) Another suggestion:

Switch out your entire victim's writing utensil collection with children's crayons (Figure 2).

! Crayon Switch

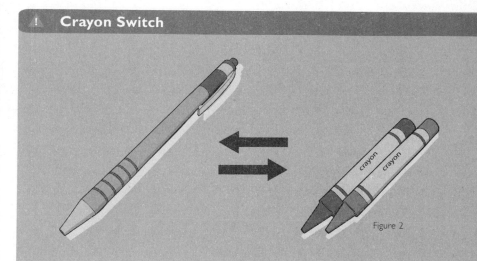

Figure 2

DIFFICULTY LEVEL 2

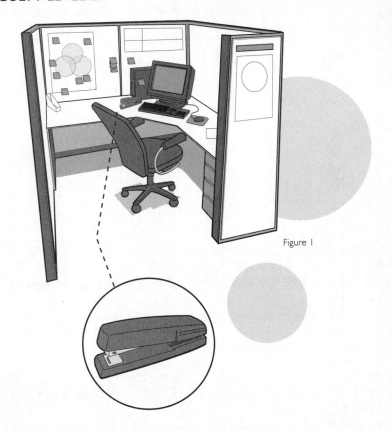

Figure 1

CLUE 1	CLUE 2	CLUE 3
Send me a file, I'll print it out Come on over and search about..	I'm 5 feet tall and green......	All this running around, you need a cup of water, 2nd from the bottom.

CLUE 4	CLUE 5	Congratulations....... you found it!
"Vend" down and look for lost change	_____ today For a better tomorrow.	at this very moment someone is in your office......cheers!

Figure 2

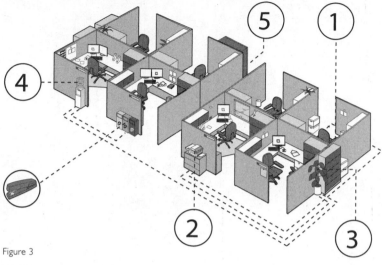

Figure 3

1) Select an item from your mark's desk that is simply indispensable.

The item you select should have personal or professional worth. It should also be worth 20 minutes of rummaging around the office trying to find it, or it's not worth your trouble to pull this prank off (Figure 1).

2) Think of some creative clues, specific to your office.

When thinking of clues, don't concentrate them in one area; instead, utilize the entire office space so your detective can entertain everyone watching (Figure 2).

3) Sit back and enjoy the show.

Try not to look involved or responsible for the clues. Keep your head down, avoid unnecessary laughter, and tell the fewest people possible (Figure 3). As soon as he suspects it was you, he will forget about your clever clues and go right to the source—you. Where is the fun in that?

Who deserves this? That coworker who always borrows your stuff and never brings it back.

TUNA SMELL

DIFFICULTY LEVEL 2

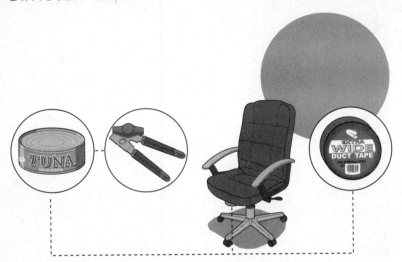

Figure 1

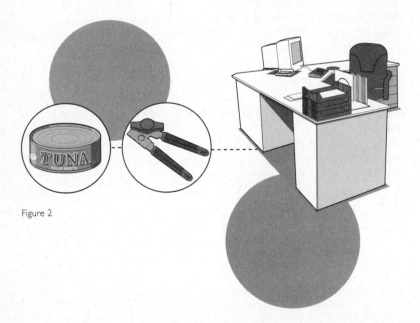

Figure 2

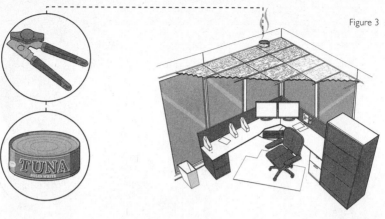

Figure 3

1) The foul smell of success.

Mystery smells in the workplace are just as much a distraction as a nuisance. Detecting an offensive odor could take hours out of someone's productive day and possibly have him question his own personal hygiene. Variations:

- **Tape a can of opened tuna under your coworker's office chair.**
  Even if your victim loves to eat tuna, the stuff still smells. Tape the can underneath the seat, and try to conceal it as best as possible, but the chances he will look under his chair are slim (Figure 1).

- **Slide a can of tuna under or in his desk.**
  This one will take him a bit longer to discover (Figure 2).

- **Upset and disrupt an entire office by placing a can of tuna in the ceiling tile.**
  The first question you need to ask is, do you like your job? If you do, then don't get caught pulling this one (Figure 3).

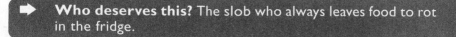

➡ **Who deserves this?** The slob who always leaves food to rot in the fridge.

DIFFICULTY LEVEL 3

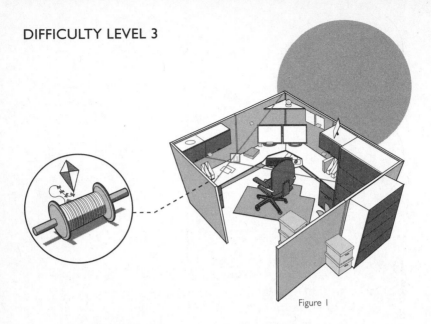

Figure 1

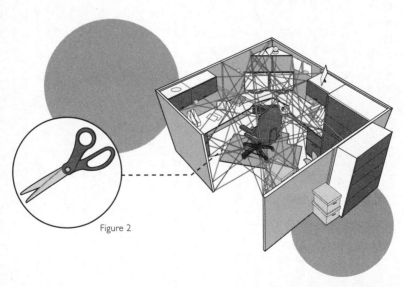

Figure 2

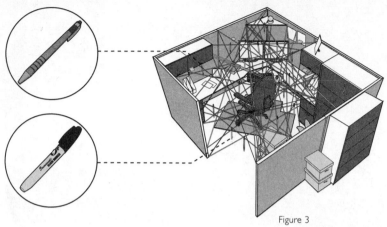

Figure 3

....

1) Arm yourself with a good-sized spool of kite string.

Begin from the rear of the office and make your way to the door. Create a web of string around the office. Tie as many things as possible to one another—the chair to the coffee mug, the ceiling tiles to the computer, the filing cabinets to the monitor . . . (Figure 1).

2) Once you've decided how much retribution your victim deserves, tie your last knot.

The amount of string you use is solely up to your judgment. Finish up and cut off the extra (Figure 2).

3) Add a few office supplies!

If you want to inconvenience your mark even more, hang the supplies up (Figure 3). This prank could be quickly executed during your lunch break or after work.

Who deserves this? The office gossip who weaves webs of half-truths.

DIFFICULTY LEVEL 1

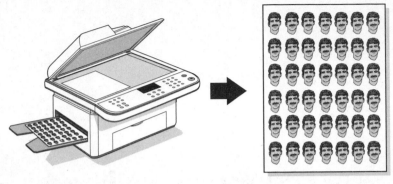

Figure 1

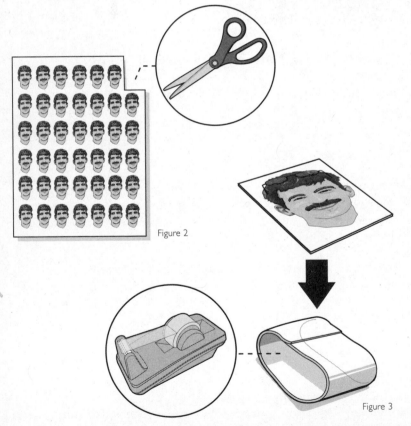

Figure 2

Figure 3

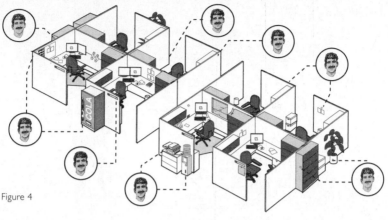

Figure 4

1) Locate a head shot of your victim.
Pictures on his or her desk, team-building photos, or the company Web site are good bets.

2) Print off multiple copies of just the head.
Using a photocopier or a computer printer, duplicate your victim's head in color or black and white (Figure 1). The number of heads you print out is up to you.

3) Cut out the individual heads.
With a scissors or a hobby knife, separate all the heads (Figure 2).

4) Prepare the little heads for quick deployment.
Assemble small tape balls, place one on the back of each head, and slide them around your fingers (Figure 3).

5) Randomly disperse the heads all over the office.
Deploy the heads on vending machines, doors, chairs, walls, signs, the ceiling, and so on (Figure 4).

➡ **Who deserves this?** The one coworker who loves to lurk around the office. Your victim will be spotting little heads for months, maybe even years, depending on your ambition.

DIFFICULTY LEVEL 2

MUST BE 18+ TO OPEN
Federal Regulation : Postal 112-3214 Section A

FROM
ADULT CITY
1663 Shore Drive
Warehouse #2
Watertown, NY
22300

TO

001
NY 22391

18+

SHIP TO POST

DEPT

PO: 114342/BRIANSANDERS

FOR

Thank you,
ADULT CITY
1663 Shore Drive
Warehouse #2
Watertown, NY
22391
Shop again..

114342

SSCC-18

Figure 1

MUST BE 18+ TO OPEN
Federal Regulation : Postal 112-3214 Section A
ADULT CITY
1663 Shore Drive Warehouse #2 Watertown, NY 22391

Figure 2

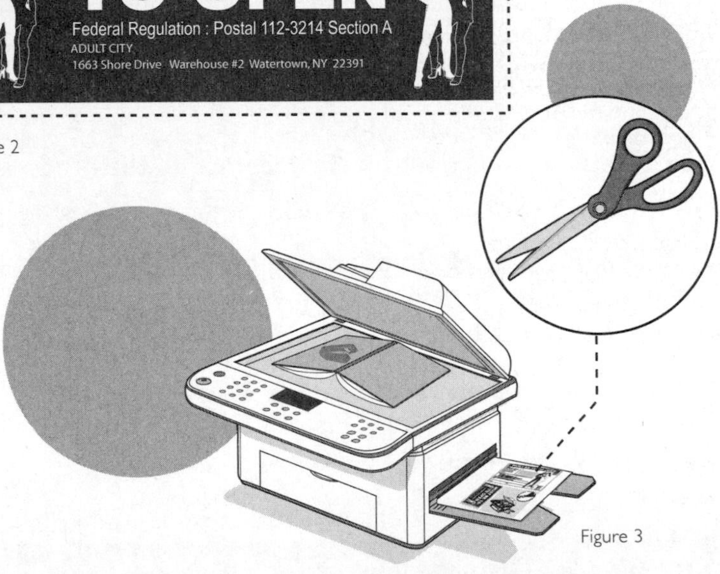

Figure 3

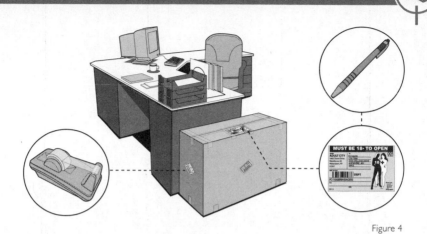

Figure 4

1) Run off the sample labels supplied on your office copy machine, or create your own.

One shipping label and 2 or 3 age warning labels will do the trick (Figures 1–3).

2) Find a very large box, one that will grab the attention of anyone entering the office.

Find an extra-large box to capture the attention of anyone who might be dropping something off or passing by the office. When it comes to the adult world of shipping, bigger is better.

3) Place the mock adult parcel in the vacationing coworker's office.

Seal the box, and possibly add some dead weight. Next, fill out the mock shipping label, and secure both labels onto the box (Figure 4).

4) Gossip about the box and speculate about its possible contents.

You need to get the word out, so start talking about the mystery box. What would possess someone to ship a box like that to work?

Who deserves this? The coworker who decides to go on vacation right in the middle of a project.

DIFFICULTY LEVEL 3

6+

Figure 1

1) Purchase several inexpensive alarm clocks.
Set the timers 10 minutes apart from one another.

2) Cleverly conceal them around your colleague's office.
You'll want to place them in areas he or she wouldn't normally look for annoying devices that make noises—for example, in the trash can, in the bottom of file boxes, taped under the chair or desk, and in the ceiling if possible (Figure 1).

2) Time for work!
Hold in the laughter as you watch your neighbor waste over an hour looking for the sound of alarms.

➡ **Who deserves this?** The coworker who always lets you know what time you got in.

(!) Another suggestion:
Electrical timers are used for aquarium lights and holiday trees. Hide a radio under your mark's desk or in the ceiling, and have the volume setting on high. As soon as the timer is activated, the radio will blast a barrage of uncontrollable audio (Figure 2).

! Electrical Timer

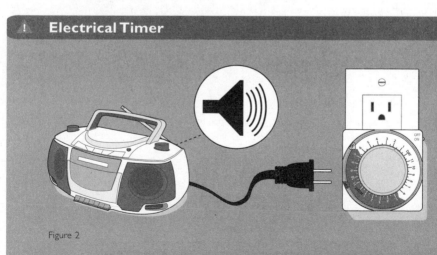

Figure 2

DIFFICULTY LEVEL 3

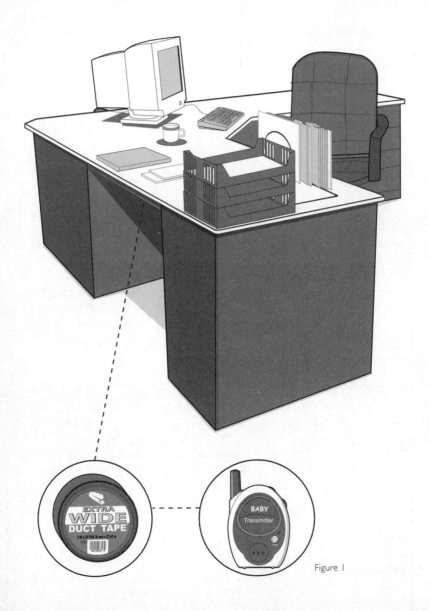

Figure 1

Figure 2

1) Set up a simple surveillance system to covertly collect classified intel.

So simple, even a baby could use! Your surveillance equipment is an ordinary set of baby monitors. You will want to install a set of fully charged batteries before concealing the units. Next, find a good monitoring area to fix the transmitter unit, such as a conference table or your target's desk (Figure 1).

2) Hide the receiver unit in your office.

Make sure your unit has a headphone jack. Hide the unit under your keyboard tray or behind your computer, and then plug in the headphones. People will assume you are listening to music or talk radio, not aware that you are transmitting information from behind enemy lines (Figure 2).

(!) Warning: possible job termination.

Security might not like your breach of privacy and lack of corporate confidentiality and this may be illegal in many states. So hide the receiver well, and never go back for the transmitter.

➡ **Who deserves this?** You, of course! If alliances have been made and the hostiles strongly outnumber you, it's time for a counterbalance.

SNOWING FLOUR

DIFFICULTY LEVEL 3

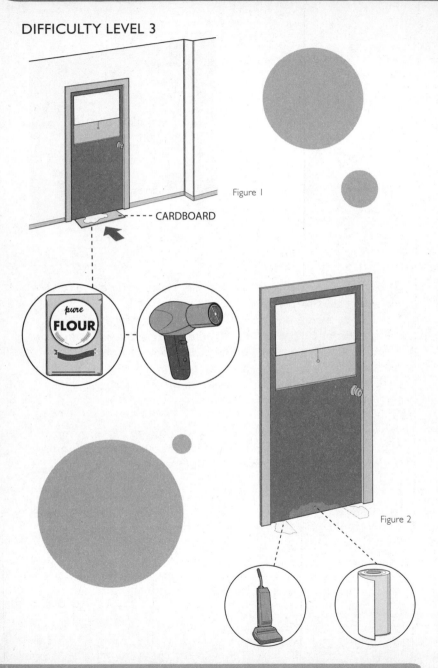

Figure 1

CARDBOARD

Figure 2

1) Pour a small pile of flour outside your victim's locked door.
You need only a small pile of flour at first. Too much will clog the door gap.

2) Use a powerful hair dryer or a can of compressed air to move the flour under the door.
The flour will become airborne and start floating around your victim's office (Figure 1).

3) Clean up any evidence outside the door and on the floor.
Vacuum up the carpet, and wipe the door of any flour residue (Figure 2).

4) Most importantly, avoid the clean-up process.
After a pound of this stuff, the office should have a nice white dusting of flour—and it's going to be messy! Do not claim responsibility.

➡ **Who deserves this?** This prank is going to be messy, so be sure your victim can take it!

FART MACHINE

DIFFICULTY LEVEL 3

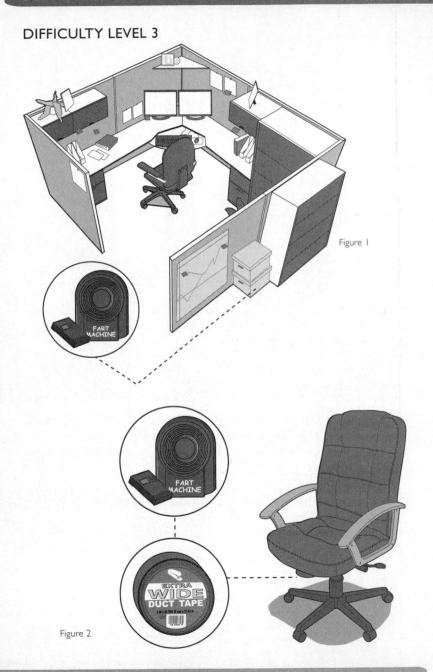

Figure 1

FART
MACHINE

FART
MACHINE

EXTRA
WIDE
DUCT TAPE

Figure 2

1) Purchase a remote-controlled electronic fart machine.

The sophisticated machines cost approximately $15 and can work up to 100 feet away.

2) Install the fart machine under your victim's chair.

Depending on the size of the device, try to conceal it as best you can under the seat (Figure 1).

3) Wait for the ideal time to begin digital flatulence.

If the boss stops in, an attractive member of the opposite sex sits, or a teleconference takes place, flip the switch.

4) Embarrass innocent bystanders.

Once your coworker comprehends what is happening and everyone has a few laughs, it is time to move the device. Set your sights on a well-traveled corridor. You will want to camouflage the machine to the best of your ability (Figure 2). Wait until two employees pass by the area simultaneously to create an embarrassing situation.

➡️ **Who deserves this?** The coworker who told everyone about your little accident in the bathroom.

(!) Another hallway suggestion:

This may seem simple, but it will scare the hell out of people! Find a large box, and wait for your prey (Figure 3). Once you sense a human presence in your vicinity, jump out!

⚠ Hallway Scare

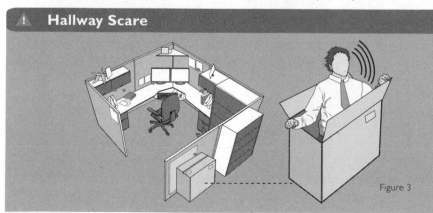

Figure 3

DIFFICULTY LEVEL 3

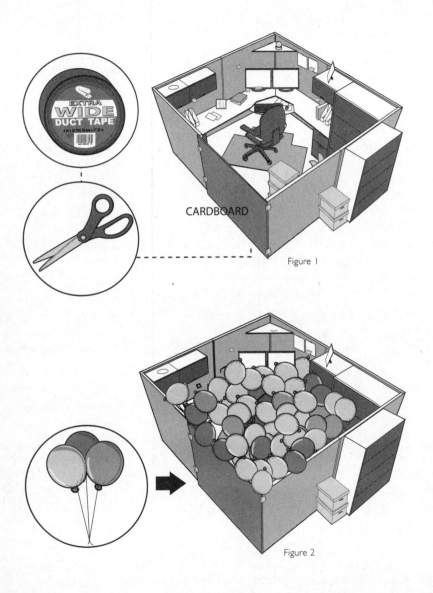

CARDBOARD

Figure 1

Figure 2

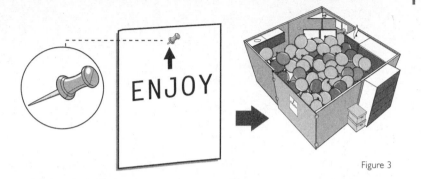

Figure 3

1) **Construct a cardboard door.**
This will help you control the balloons in your victim's cubicle (Figure 1).

2) **Begin to inflate hundreds of balloons.**
This is a great job for everyone in your area to pitch in. The morning of the prank, walk around and give everybody a handful of deflated balloons (Figure 2).

3) **Fill up your victim's cubicle.**
With office participation, you should be able to fill the entire cube to the top of the walls.

4) **Place an easy-to-see note at the entrance of your creation.**
One suggestion is "ENJOY" with an arrow pointing to a tack (Figure 3).

➡ Who deserves this? That administrative assistant who won't stop passing around birthday cards for everyone to sign.

(!) Another suggestion:
If you want to go above and beyond, fill a few balloons with water and mix them in with the others. You could also have the balloons custom printed with your targeted victim's face.

DIFFICULTY LEVEL 3

Figure 1

1) This prank is pretty simple.
Blanket the entire cubicle with small yellow sticky-notes (Figure 1).

2) Everything is free after 5 o'clock.
Not only is this easy to execute, but it's dirt cheap and possibly even free, depending on your supply cabinet.

3) Avoid clean-up!
However, on the flip side, clean-up is a real pain in the ass, so make sure your victim won't go insane and fire you.

Who deserves this? That boss who needs a little hint about all the annoying little tasks you keep being assigned.

(!) Another suggestion:
Does your mark have a huge white wall not being adequately used? If you answered yes, then it's time to create a personal poster. This creation involves time and skill. You have two choices. The first option is to use a computer and grid out your face, then print it (Figure 2). The second option is to use the copier to blow up an image, cut it out into little puzzle pieces, and tape them up in disarray for your victim to solve.

Personal Poster

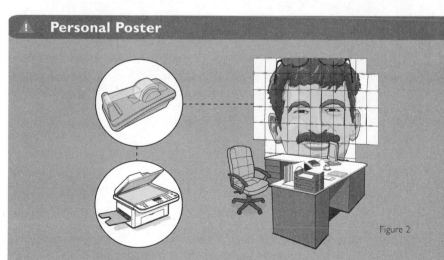

Figure 2

DIFFICULTY LEVEL 3

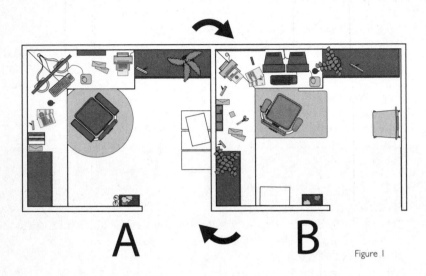

Figure 1

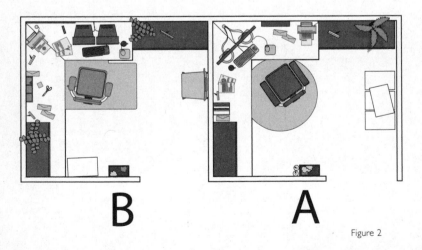

Figure 2

1) Wait around until everyone leaves the office.
You may want to run out and grab some food, then return when everyone has left.

2) Begin switching the contents of the two offices.
Start by placing all the small items in cardboard boxes to avoid mixing up their stuff. After that, proceed with the larger items. This whole process will take several hours, so you may want to find a partner to help (Figures 1 and 2).

3) The following morning, play dumb.
Just act natural and surprised, unless it's obvious that you're the guilty party.

➡ **Who deserves this?** If you find yourself facing two worthy adversaries at work, this is the prank for you.

(!) Another suggestion:
Remove all the items out of your victim's space, and place them in a supply closet (Figure 3).

Janitor's Closet

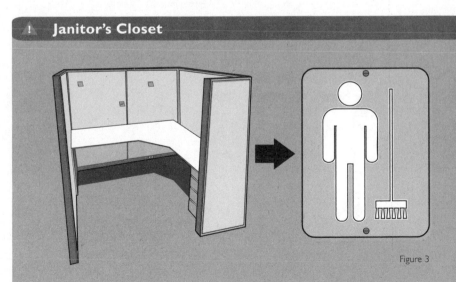

Figure 3

DIFFICULTY LEVEL 4

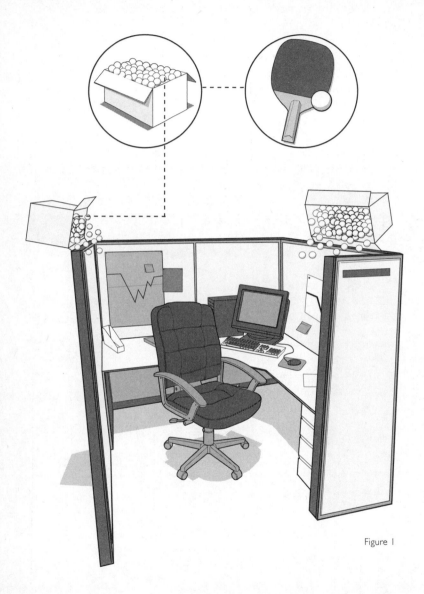

Figure 1

1) Stock up on boxes of Ping-Pong balls.
You'll need several hundred Ping-Pong balls to complete this prank (Figure1). Remove them from their packages, and hide all the balls in boxes in your mark's office under the desk until they're needed.

2) Team up with your office neighbors.
Recruit a few more corporate commandos to help you surround the selected target's cubicle. Wait for him to be on the phone with an important client.

3) Wait for the signal, then release the balls.
When ready, give the signal and watch hundreds of little white balls pour out of the boxes and cascade into the clean cube (Figure 2). Remember to maintain the element of surprise when attacking.

Figure 2

Who deserves this? The dude in the next cube who is nice enough to point out how much crap you seem to have lying around.

DIFFICULTY LEVEL 4

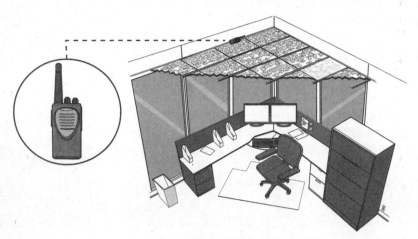

Figure 1

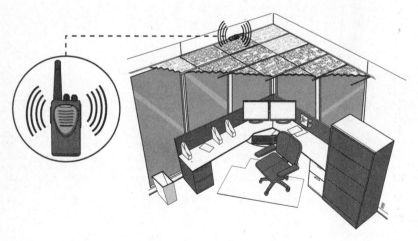

Figure 2

1) You will need one set of portable two-way radios.
Make sure to test them before trying this out.

2) Gain access to the office ceiling.
Best to do this before or after work hours.

3) Place one of the radios up in the rafters.
After you've fully charged the unit, switch the device on (Figure 1).

4) Begin transmitting gospel from a secure location in the office.
Music, daily news, scripture—anything that will distract your mark (Figure 2).

➡ **Who deserves this?** That chick who planned her entire wedding from the cube next to yours.

(!) Another suggestion:
Sick of that damned ring tone? Remove her cell phone from her desk and place it up in the ceiling. Once it is in position, begin calling it periodically throughout the day (Figure 3).

! Ceiling Cell

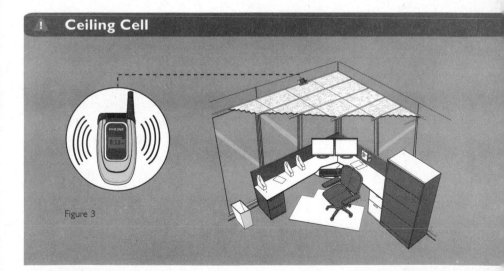

Figure 3

DIFFICULTY LEVEL 5

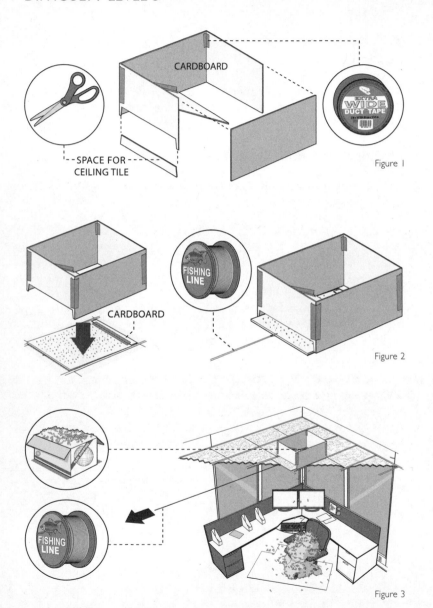

CARDBOARD

SPACE FOR CEILING TILE

Figure 1

CARDBOARD

Figure 2

Figure 3

1) Locate the ceiling tile directly above your victim's chair.

2) Construct the cardboard housing to hold the packing peanuts.
After a few quick measurements, begin to construct the holding area for the packing peanuts (Figure 1). The newly constructed cardboard box should be larger than the ceiling tile. If you're working within a smaller area, a cardboard slope is recommended to increase the amount of packing peanuts in the tile opening.

3) Determine the direction you wish to pull the tile, and prepare the tile for the slide.
Remove cardboard material from the box wall to allow the tile to pass underneath the wall when being pulled (Figure 1).

4) Fasten a cord, rope, or fishing line to the end of the ceiling tile you plan on pulling.
Then lift the tile slightly out of the drop-ceiling groove. Now, you will need to make the ceiling tile gap less obvious. Do this by attaching a piece of white cardboard to the tile, using office tape (Figure 2).

5) Install the newly constructed cardboard housing in the ceiling, and fill it with packing peanuts.
After the cardboard housing is installed, fill housing with peanuts by removing the tile next to the housing.

6) Wait for your victim, then slowly pull the line.
Gently pull the line from a covert location (Figure 3).

Who deserves this? The guy who gives everyone nicknames because he can't remember names.

DIFFICULTY LEVEL 5

Figure 1

ATTENTION
These premises are under
constant TV Surveillance.
24 Hour recording
in progress!

Figure 2

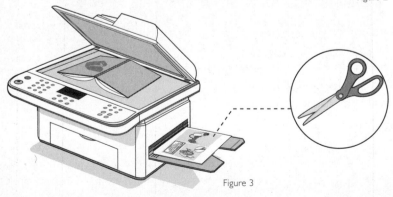

Figure 3

Figure 4

1) Purchase a fake security camera.
An artificial camera can range from $4.95 to $50, depending on material and quality (Figure 1). Models with 24-hour flashing LED are recommended. These models are wireless and require only two AA batteries.

2) These premises are under constant TV surveillance!
Adding signage will alert your audience that a camera is present (Figure 2). If you would like to use the sign provided, just place the page on the photocopier and print it (Figure 3).

3) Quick assembly; no wires needed.
These cameras install easily with a standard screwdriver (Figure 4). Once up, this camera will deter office robbery, and desk vandalism, and will tame your mark's office pranking.

4) Tell your coworker that apparently someone complained about his lack of company spirit.

➡ **Who deserves this?** That newbie who is already worried about being fired.

(!) Warning: possible job termination.
Security might not like your planting fake security cameras around the facility.

DIFFICULTY LEVEL 5

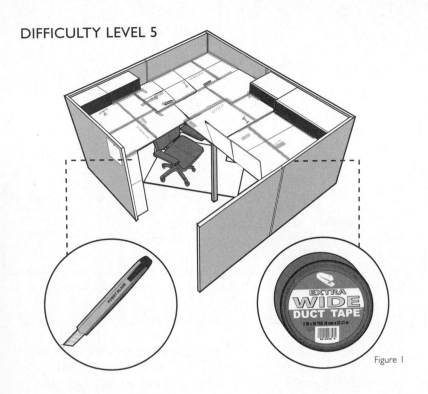

Figure 1

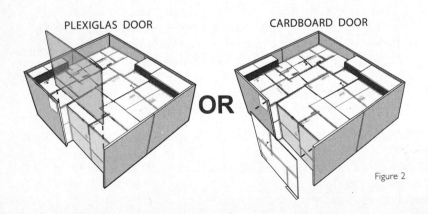

PLEXIGLAS DOOR

OR

CARDBOARD DOOR

Figure 2

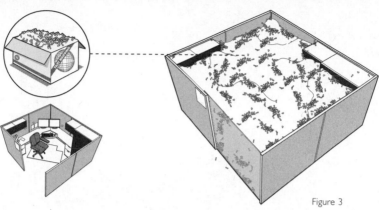

Figure 3

1) Accumulate a large amount of cardboard, and start constructing.

Gather large sheets of cardboard to create a structure a few inches lower than the cubicle wall. Use the office chair as a load-bearing wall for the center of the structure while taping the rest together (Figure 1).

2) Fancy Plexiglas or poor man's cardboard door?

This will be the most expensive addition to your masterpiece. Purchase one or two pieces of Plexiglas to cover the door (Figure 2). This will give the illusion that the whole cubicle is filled with peanuts. Your office may have a few large framed posters hanging around; these are a great resource for free Plexiglas. If you're short on cash, you can also use more cardboard instead of the Plexiglas.

3) Fill her up!

Frost the top of the cubicle with packing peanuts. Spread them around to blanket all the cardboard, and don't forget to completely fill the doorway (Figure 3).

 Who deserves this? Anyone on an extended vacation, questionable sick day, boondoggle business trip—and, of course, anyone who irritates you!

BONUS

Figure 1

1) Acquire high-strength industrial Velcro.
The Velcro should have adhesive backing for easy use.

2) Randomly cover the wall next to your victim's desk with his or her supplies and equipment.
Anything and everything goes. When completed, it will look as if gravity is playing an awful game (Figure 1).

➡ **Who deserves this?** The coworker who wears stylish Velcro shoes.

DESKTOP DISASTERS 2

PAY BACK

DIFFICULTY LEVEL 1

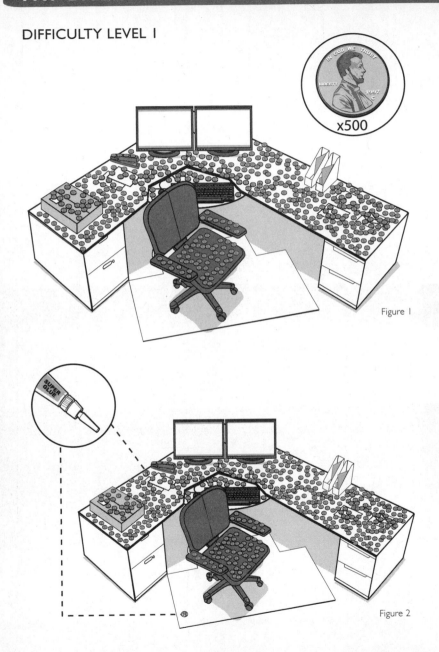

Figure 1

Figure 2

1) Quick deployment, perfect for a preemptive attack.

Quietly stationed at your desk, you maintain visual surveillance. Once your suspected stingy mark clears the designated area, advance.

2) Open up the rolls of coins and begin to litter his or her selected workspace.

Costing only a few dollars, this prank is very cheap and very effective (Figure 1). With extra time and for extra fun, you can glue down some coins (Figure 2).

3) Once you've completed your mission, quietly withdraw back into the cabinet jungle.

After only a few minutes, your mission is complete. You have sent a very powerful message. Pay up, or experience harsh payback.

➡ **Who deserves this?** That employee who borrows money but always forgets to pay it back.

(!) Another suggestion:

Placing innumerable paper clips on someone's desk (Figure 3) is both juvenile and very unprofessional—but isn't that the point?

! Paper Clip Desk

x400

Figure 3

PAPER CLIP CHAIN

DIFFICULTY LEVEL I

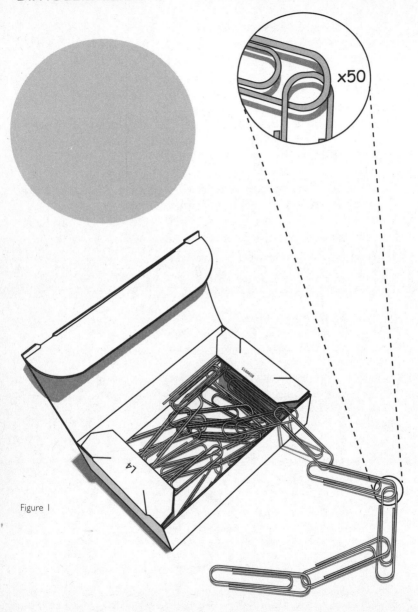

x50

Figure I

1) Loop your coworker's paper clips together to form a chain.

Once the whole box has been transformed into a chain, put them back in the box as if nothing had ever happened (Figure 1). This will definitely irritate your victim as soon as he reaches in for just one paper clip.

➡ **Who deserves this?** Anyone having an especially stressful day and just needs one more thing to go wrong before totally losing it.

(!) A few more suggestions:

Other ingenious ways to torment a defenseless box of paper clips (Figures 2–5).

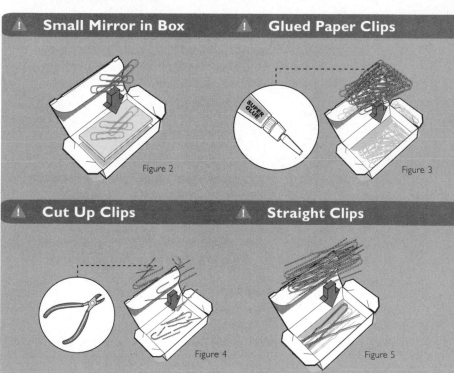

! Small Mirror in Box

Figure 2

! Glued Paper Clips

Figure 3

! Cut Up Clips

Figure 4

! Straight Clips

Figure 5

SALTED PENS

DIFFICULTY LEVEL 1

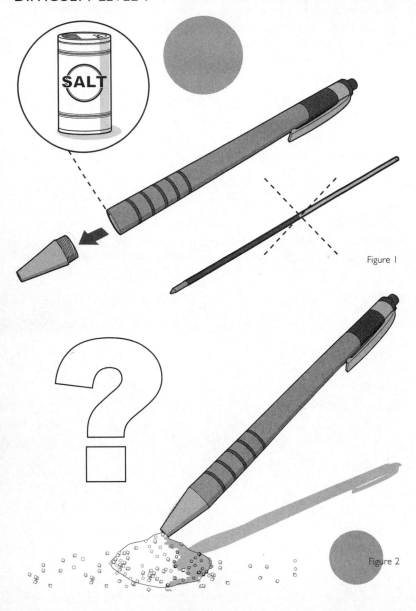

Figure 1

Figure 2

1) Everybody hates when a pen doesn't work!
Not all pranks have to be elaborate and expensive. Some are well designed just to be annoying.

2) Remove the ink and the mechanical guts from the pen housing.
Do not discard these items. You most likely will be returning them once you have frustrated your mark (Figure 1).

3) Once you've emptied the housing fill it with sugar or salt, then reassemble the pen.
A fine sugar or salt will work best. After the pen is assembled, place all the salted pens back in their original location.

4) Your pen pal will be unaware of the salty insides until he or she decides to start using it.
To his or her amazement, salt will pour out of the tip instead of ink (Figure 2).

➡️ **Who deserves this?** The coworker who contributes to noise pollution with excessive pen tapping.

(!) Another suggestion:
Two options here. The first is to fill the pen with a smelly bologna or some other type of foul-smelling food product (Figure 3). The second is to rub all the pens down with an onion so the stench transfers to the victim's fingers.

⚠️ Pen Stench

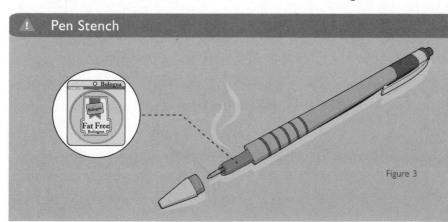

Figure 3

DIFFICULTY LEVEL 1

Figure 1

CONDOM
ULTRA PLEASURE

Figure 2

1) Office romance is in the air.
Companies try to ban interoffice dating among their employees, but lust can be a wild animal (Figure 1).

**2) You will need a few props to authenticate a believ-
able desk hook-up.**
Stop by a second-hand store and purchase some underwear,
a few socks, and whatever else you can think of. A condom,
lipstick, a few napkins, and some munchies also help.

3) Set the stage, and reposition a majority of the items on your mark's desk.

You will want to create enough room suitable for two people passionately making love. Imagine a wild scenario taking place, monitor possibly kicked, pencils spilled, and someone sliding off all the desk contents to the floor (Figure 2).

4) Disperse your purchased props.

Now add the spent condom, a few random dress socks, someone's underwear, and, of course, torn nylons.

5) They might actually buy it!

Depending on the number of pranks being played, they might actually believe someone hooked up.

➡ **Who deserves this?** The dude who busted you hooking up with the assistant at the office party.

(!) Another suggestion:

This is a great prank for in the office as well executing from a satellite office. Anonymously send flowers to your mark with a special message (Figure 3). Once they've been received, someone is going to have a very uncomfortable day.

Flowers From Who

FLOWERS — SOMEONE THINKS YOUR SPECIAL

I LOVE WORKING LATE NIGHTS WITH YOU

FLOWERS — SOMEONE THINKS YOUR SPECIAL

YOU LOOKED VERY SEXY YESTERDAY

FLOWERS — SOMEONE THINKS YOUR SPECIAL

THESE SMELL ALMOST AS GOOD AS YOU DO

-YOUR E-MAIL FRIEND

FLOWERS — SOMEONE THINKS YOUR SPECIAL

SORRY ABOUT THE NEWS

Figure 3

DIFFICULTY LEVEL I

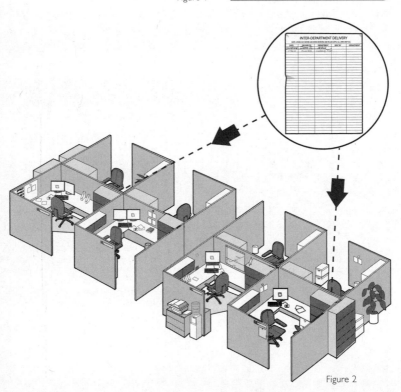

Figure 1

Figure 2

1) Who the hell sent this?

Undergarments, letters from secret admirers, and other random, and personal paraphernalia are the last things you expect from the interoffice mail services.

2) Purchase some undergarments at a second-hand store.

Bra, underwear, nylons, or whatever else you can get your hands on for a few dollars (Figure 1).

3) Make sure the interoffice envelope does not have your name on it.

You don't want anyone—especially human resources—contacting you for sending a thong in the mail.

4) Send the obscene package to your mark.

It's best if you observe his or her reaction. If your mark falls for it, keep it up throughout the month (Figure 2).

Who deserves this? The office Romeo.

(!) Another suggestion:

Take a blank CD and write "porn" on it. Interoffice mail it to your next-door cubicle neighbor (Figure 3). Or, better yet, put it into his or her CD drive, so your mark will be shocked when he or she decides to load a new CD.

Interoffice Weekly Porn

Figure 3

TAPE DISPENSER

DIFFICULTY LEVEL I

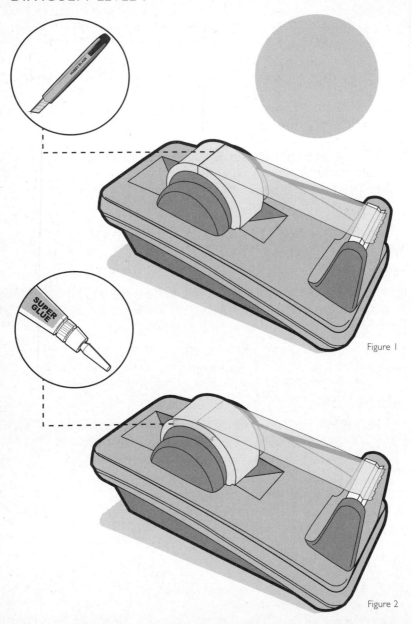

Figure 1

Figure 2

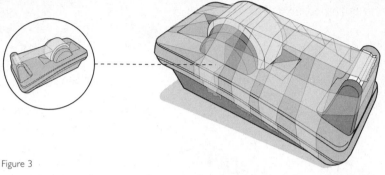

Figure 3

• •

1) Three ways to sabotage your mark's tape dispenser.

You've got to love tape; it's quick, simple, and easy to use, just like these pranks.

- **Cut the roll all the way down to the plastic wheel.**
  Every time your victim uses the tape, he or she will have to fingernail the next piece. This will get old real quick; in fact, don't be surprised if he or she just discards the roll (Figure 1).

- **The tape roll that wouldn't roll.**
  This can go two ways. The first is to glue the roll together so the tape is useless. The second method is to glue the roll to the dispenser so the dispenser is useless. Your choice (Figure 2)!

- **Tape the tape—why not?**
  Cocoon your mark's tape in a tightly taped ball (Figure 3).

➡ Who deserves this? Anyone who steals your tape dispenser.

DIFFICULTY LEVEL I

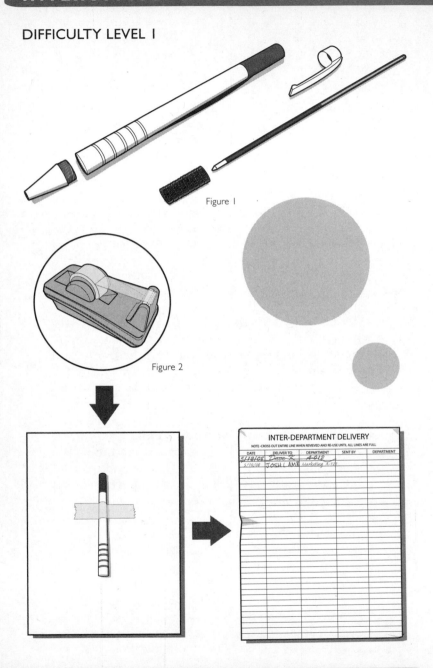

Figure I

Figure 2

INTER-DEPARTMENT DELIVERY

NOTE - CROSS OUT ENTIRE LINE WHEN REVIEWED AND RE-USE UNTIL ALL LINES ARE FULL

DATE	DELIVER TO	DEPARTMENT	SENT BY	DEPARTMENT
5/18/08	Dave Z	A-018		
5/10/08	JOSH LAMB	Marketing A-12B		

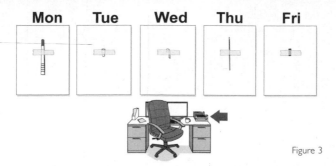

Mon	Tue	Wed	Thu	Fri

Figure 3

1) Limited-edition ballpoint pen; are you crazy?
It is rather amusing when someone spends a fortune on a simple ballpoint pen. Maybe he is unaware you have a supply room full of practically free pens.

2) Swipe the extravagant pen when no one is looking, and disassemble it.
You're not stealing it, because you plan on returning it soon. Disassemble the pen into 5 parts if possible. It is essential that you go undetected (Figure 1).

3) You will also need to possess five interoffice envelopes.
It is very important that your name is not on the envelopes. In fact, this is a good opportunity to frame another office nemesis by forging his signature on the last recipient to receive the envelopes.

4) Prepare your parcels.
Securely tape each part of the pen to a standard-size paper, and place them in the interoffice envelopes (Figure 2).

5) Now mail each envelope in sequential order over the next 5 days.
Your mark's emotions will change during this period. He will be upset when he suspects he's lost his pen. However, he will be completely confused when the first parcel shows up (Figure 3).

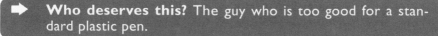

Who deserves this? The guy who is too good for a standard plastic pen.

DIFFICULTY LEVEL I

Figure I

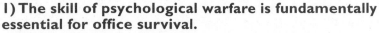

1) The skill of psychological warfare is fundamentally essential for office survival.
Knowing people's hot buttons can sometimes be just as effective as knowing all the answers.

2) You need one random book, one sticky note, one writing utensil, and 20 seconds of your time.
It's simple. Write a message on a sticky note to encourage your victim to some pointless recommended reading (Figure 1). He or she won't know who left the note, but will only assume that it must have been the boss. I recommend leaving the note with only minutes of work left, so time to question the note will be short lived.

➡ **Who deserves this?** The guy who always seems to be busy but doesn't do any work.

(!) Another suggestion:
A few more phrases you can leave on your mark's desk in passing (Figure 2).

Please don't pick your nose at work,
it's gross!

Your fly is undone....a friend

Security called..something about the
parking lot ?

Stop by my office when you get in

You missed the conference call
this morning!

Please DO NOT steal my damn stapler!
Last warning!

Looks like you sat in something...   Figure 2

CHAIR PULL

DIFFICULTY LEVEL 2

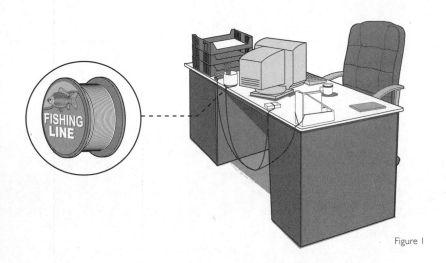

Figure 1

Figure 2

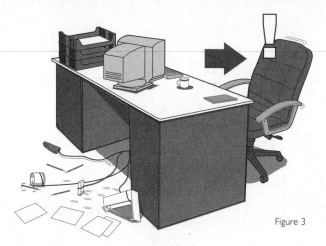

Figure 3

1) **Select a few items on your victim's desk to place on the back edge.**
Items should be able to take a 3-foot fall with out breaking. Pencils, paper clip container, paper holder, and a fully filled alphabetized Rolodex are a few good choices.

2) **Attach fishing line to the items you have selected.**
Clear fishing line is less obvious than colored (Figure 1).

3) **Run the lines under the desk, and tie them together.**
It is important that all the lines have the same tension when you merge them into one so that when your mark pulls his or her chair back, all the selected items launch at once.

4) **Push the chair into the desk, and attach the remaining line to the chair.**
Your unsuspecting victim will never notice your mischievous act once the lines are concealed (Figure 2).

5) **Time for your victim to have a seat.**
He or she will casually pull out the chair, only to be startled when items begin to launch off the back of the desk (Figure 3).

 Who deserves this? Anyone who is more organized than you.

GRAPHITE DESK

DIFFICULTY LEVEL 2

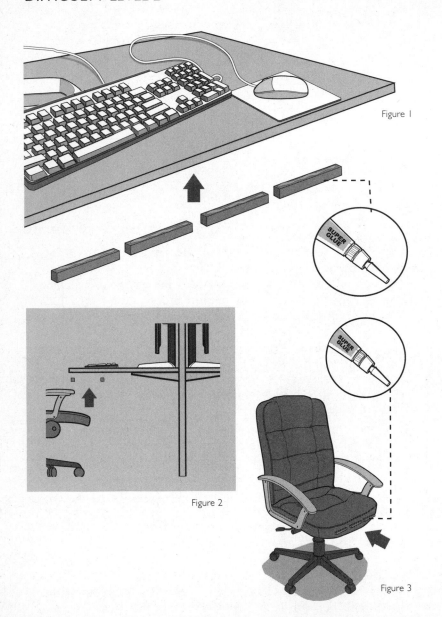

Figure 1

Figure 2

Figure 3

1) What is a graphite stick?
Graphite sticks are generally used for large pencil drawings. You can purchase them at most art and craft stores and all art supply stores. Substitute paperless crayons and/or chalk if graphite is unavailable.

2) Study your victim's seating arrangement before executing.
It is important to take note of certain areas that brush or rub up against your mark's clothing (Figure 1).

3) Glue or tape the sticks under the desk.
Place the sticks at the edge of the desk in the location of the knees and/or thigh area (Figure 2).

4) Next, attack your victim's chair with more graphite sticks.
These sticks will be most effective. Place them at the edge of the chair and/or around the armrest (Figure 3).

5) Your victim will be dumbfounded when he starts spotting black marks on his clothing.

Who deserves this? Your associate who can't seem to eat lunch without getting it all over his or her clothes.

(!) Another suggestion:
Deteriorating broccoli gives off a mysterious smell of decay. Duct-tape a few pieces under your victim's desk after acquiring them from the corporate cafeteria salad bar (Figure 4).

Broccoli Stench

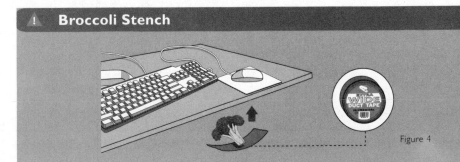

Figure 4

DIFFICULTY LEVEL 2

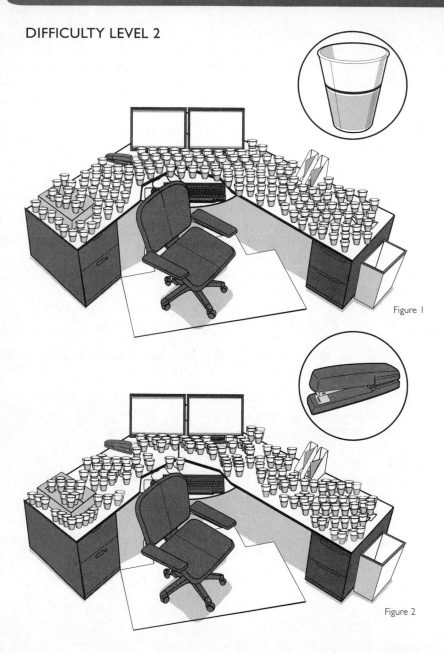

Figure 1

Figure 2

Figure 3

....

1) Everything looks good in multiples!
And if that statement holds true, this operation is going to
be a true masterpiece.

**2) Start by blanketing your target's whole desk with
paper cups.**
Smuggle a few hundred free cups out of the break room.
Tightly place the cups next to each other (Figure 1).

**3) Intensify your masterpiece by stapling the cups
together.**
Using a standard office stapler, start stapling all the cups
together. This will add to the complexity of the clean-up
(Figure 2).

4) To add insult to injury, fill the cups with H_2O.
Your victim will find it nearly impossible to clean up this
water contraption (Figure 3). This network of paper cups, sta-
ples, and water will surely disrupt anyone's work day. Don't feel
bad—they probably had it coming anyway. Payback is a bitch!

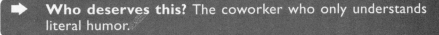

➡ **Who deserves this?** The coworker who only understands
literal humor.

DIFFICULTY LEVEL 2

Vulgar Language

Dress Code Infractions

Smoke Break Abuse

Messy Workstation

Inappropriate Internet Use

Customer Complaints

Number of Personal Days

Inappropriate Phone Use

Figure 1

1) The human resources department is a well-equipped regiment ready to strike at any time.
As much as they service you, they are also very capable of dismissing your services. Your mark is probably a perfect employee; however, no one likes to get a warning from HR.

2) Conduct surveillance to study your mark's work habits.

Watch your victim, and decide which daily activity you wish to exploit. The corporate conduct code tolerates low levels of insubordination, but it's your job to fabricate and exaggerate them. For example, your mark takes only a few personal phone calls during work. By your standards, that merits a full-fledged HR warning. He may also surf the Internet only a few times a day, yet you can misinform him of documented hours of personal Internet use and the prohibited visitation of adult Web sites.

3) Using company stationery, forge a professional letter reprimanding your victim.

Beware—this is the step in which a simple joke and permanent termination blur. Using company stationery to forge a letter could be catastrophic to your employment, so proceed with caution. Once you've written the letter send it using interoffice mail (Figure 1). You might want to add that this is only a warning, however; it will be written up in your victim's permanent record, and his professional understanding is appreciated.

Who deserves this? Anyone who treats HR as if it's a weekly therapy session.

(!) Another suggestion:

Using corporate stationery, forge a letter to your target outlining his upcoming exit interview (Figure 2). Be sure to include his full name, job title, and mail stop for authenticity.

! Exit Interview

Mr. Smith
Mail stop 1121

We have received your letter of resignation and are in the process of setting up your exit interview. Please contact your HR representative to confirm the appointment.

Thank you,
Jane Doe

Figure 2

DIFFICULTY LEVEL 2

Figure 1

Figure 2

Figure 3

....

1) Nice photo collection!
Kids playing, wedding photos, last weekend's fishing trip—
your associate has them all.

2) Using the office photocopier, duplicate your mark's face in multiple sizes.
You will need an array of sizes for different-scaled heads in
your mark's photos (Figure 1).

3) Cut out all your mark's heads and tape them onto the photos.
After you have removed all the paper, prepare them for the
photos. Using a very small amount of tape, attach them to
various photos on the desk (Figure 2).

4) Once you've got the system down, continue until all the photos have your mark's face on them.
The job isn't complete until you've covered every photo in
the office (Figure 3). Even pets aren't off limits.

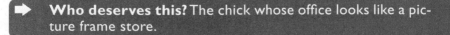

Who deserves this? The chick whose office looks like a picture frame store.

DARK COFFEE BBs

DIFFICULTY LEVEL 3

CUP 1

CUP 2

Figure 1

CUP 2

CUP 1

400-600 PIECES

600 PREMIUM GRADE BBs

BBs

Figure 2

Figure 3

1) This prank will require two paper coffee cups.
Remove the bottom of Cup A and the bottom half of Cup B, using a hobby knife (Figure 1).

2) Glue A and B together.
Glue the bottom half of B upside down in A, using a hot glue gun (Figure 2). It is important to seal the two cups together so they are watertight.

3) Fill the bottom of the cup with BBs.
Flip the newly assembled cup upside down. Fill the bottom of the cup with as many BBs as the space allows (Figure 3).

4) Slide your trap in front of your target's keyboard.
Your next step will be tricky. Place a piece of thin cardboard over the newly poured BBs. Apply pressure on the cardboard, and slowly flip the cup over. Now, in front of your mark's keyboard, cautiously slide the cardboard from underneath the cup (Figure 4).

5) Pour the appropriate amount of dark coffee to cover the false bottom.
As soon as your victim attempts to remove the cup, the BBs will come pouring out the bottom.

 Who deserves this? The over-caffeinated assistant who brings her Thursday voice to work on Monday mornings.

DIFFICULTY LEVEL 3

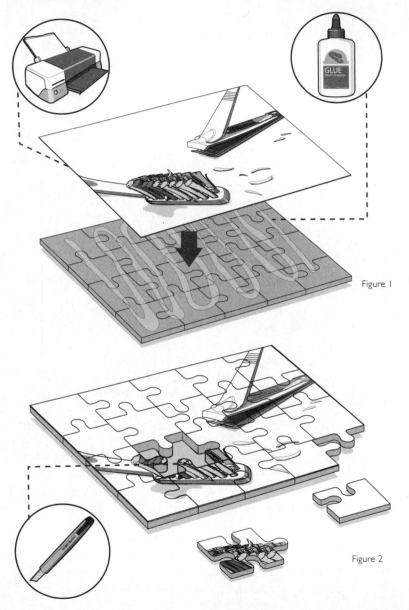

Figure 1

Figure 2

Figure 3

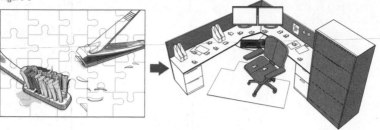

....

1) It is very important to keep the lines of communication in your office open.
However, sometimes you may find it difficult to professionally convey a difficult message without jeopardizing your political stance in the workplace. Here is an abnormal way to do just that!

2) Acquire a kid's jigsaw puzzle with approximately 15 to 20 pieces.
The puzzle should be no larger than the size of a standard piece of paper.

3) Write or photograph the information you want to tactfully broadcast to your target.
Print out the message at approximately the same size as the jigsaw puzzle. Then glue the page on the assembled jigsaw puzzle. Be cautious about the amount of adhesive you use; try to avoid gluing the actual jigsaw puzzle pieces together (Figure 1).

4) Next, creatively cut out each jigsaw piece to create a custom puzzle.
This will take time and skill, but the final product is definitely worth it. The best method is to cut out an individual piece, then proceed to the next (Figure 2).

5) Disperse the custom puzzle pieces around your target's work area.
Slowly your target will assemble the puzzling code and discover the unexpected (Figure 3).

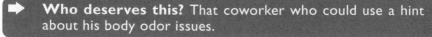

Who deserves this? That coworker who could use a hint about his body odor issues.

DIFFICULTY LEVEL 3

Figure 1

1) It is just common decency never to mess with another person's office chair.
They've sat in it hundreds of times, never really thinking anything of it, and then you come along.

- **A damp seat is an uncomfortable feeling.**
  There are several ways to execute this. The first and most obvious is to just pour water on the seat. When your victim walks away, nonchalantly stroll over and dump the water. The second way requires more patience and artfulness. Using your finger, push down on the fabric until you've made a fairly large indent. Next, slowly pour the water where your finger is still pushing. The

trick is to have the cushion, not the fabric, absorb the water. This will almost be impossible to detect by the human eye (Figure 1).

- **Using tape, fasten a well-scented air freshener under the seat.**
Eventually the smell will be overwhelming (Figure 1).

- **Using super glue, adhere the wheels of the chair to halt mobility.**
Before executing, determine the cost of the chair, and use your best judgment (Figure 1).

- **Have a few screws loose?**
Real simple—begin to start unscrewing everything. You will want to unscrew almost to the point of disassembly (Figure 1).

➡ **Who deserves this?** Anyone who has a better chair than you.

(!) Two quick suggestions:
The first is adding a food smell to the chair. Pickles or pickle juice will do the job with the best of them (Figure 2). The second is a quick readjustment every day for a week (Figure 3).

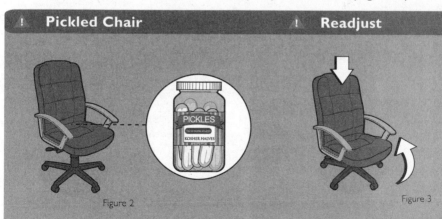

! **Pickled Chair**   ! **Readjust**

Figure 2

Figure 3

DIFFICULTY LEVEL 3

EMPTY

Figure 1

H_2O

Figure 2

Figure 3

1) Place an empty upside-down plastic cup in front of your victim's keyboard Monday through Thursday.
It's simple—just walk by and place an empty paper cup in front of your victim's keyboard. Do this Monday through Thursday (Figure 1).

2) Now it's Friday. Time to implement your trap!
Using the same type of cup you used during the week, fill this one up with water. Place a thin piece of plastic on top of the cup. Then, holding it tightly in place, rotate the cup around without spilling too much water. Next, place the tightly covered cup in front of the desk, and slowly slide out the bottom plastic. A small amount of spillage is expected. Wipe the surface around the cup to avoid detection (Figure 2).

3) Who the hell keeps leaving empty cups in my office?
Your victim will think this one is empty also. If all goes well, the water should have formed a bond and stayed hidden under the cup. Your unsuspecting victim will think nothing of it and just discard the cup, as in his previous encounters. However, this time he'll be surprised as water comes pouring out of the cup all over his workspace (Figure 3). You may want to move important paperwork on his desk during Friday's setup.

Who deserves this? The coworker who takes the last cup of coffee and doesn't make a new pot.

DIFFICULTY LEVEL 3

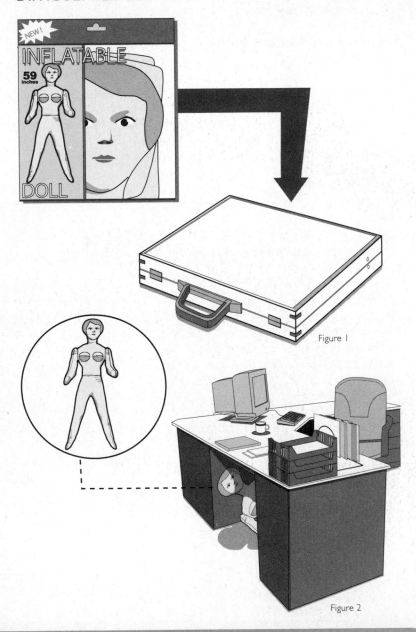

Figure 1

Figure 2

Figure 3

1) This is very important: don't get caught carrying in the inflatable doll!
Talk about rumors spreading and losing what little professional reputation you may have. If a staff member inadvertently sees you with an inflatable doll and doesn't know about the joke, people are going to talk, so hide it (Figure 1).

2) Confirm that everyone has left the office, and then inflate your life-size doll.
Out of sight, begin inflating the doll. It would be a very awkward situation if someone happened to see you now, so keep the doll low and out of sight.

3) Place your inflatable friend under your mark's desk.
Stuff it underneath the desk, and then slide the chair back into place (Figure 2).

4) Camped out under your victim's desk, your doll will wait until it is discovered.
Your victim will be not only surprised, but also completely embarrassed when he has to dispose of the thing (Figure 3).

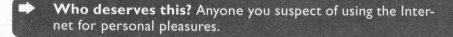

Who deserves this? Anyone you suspect of using the Internet for personal pleasures.

DIFFICULTY LEVEL 3

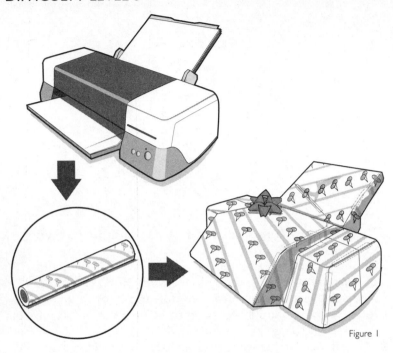

Figure 1

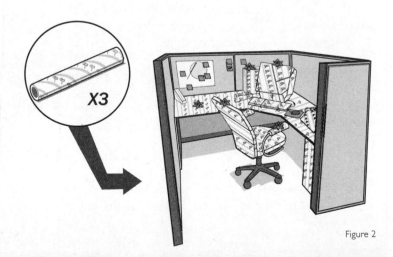

Figure 2

1) You're making a list and checking it twice, going to find out who's naughty and nice.
In this case, naughty boys and girls do get gifts.

2) Purchase 3 to 4 rolls of holiday wrap.
Predetermine the approximate amount of square footage you will need.

3) Using company tape, begin to cover all your victim's office equipment.
Monitors, computer towers, printers, scanners, keyboard, mouse, and his chair are just a few of the items you could blanket in holiday cheer (Figure 1).

4) After the major components are covered, target the less important accessories.
Proceed to everything else on the desk (Figure 2).

➡ **Who deserves this?** The coworker who loves to give personal holiday gifts.

(!) Another suggestion:
Some of the major sports franchises have licensed gift-wrap. If your team has just humiliated your friend's favorite team, celebrate by wrapping the whole cube (Figure 3).

⚠ Sports Rival

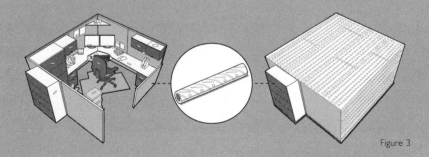

Figure 3

FOILED OFFICE

DIFFICULTY LEVEL 4

Figure 1

Figure 2

1) Purchase 2 or 3 rolls of aluminum foil.
The amount of square footage needed is determined by the amount of foiling you plan to do.

2) Foil the desk first, but first move all the contents to the floor.
If you can't remember where everything goes, make a simple drawing to assist you when you have to place all the items back on the desk. Once the items are removed, start laying individual sheets of aluminum foil neatly across your victim's desk. You may want to use tape on the underside of the desk to hold the foil in place (Figure 1).

3) Next, individually wrap all the contents, and place them back on the desk.
Pictures, desk lamp, stapler, tape dispenser, business card holder, nameplate, and anything else your victim had displayed on the desk. Thumbtacks and paper clips should also be considered; your attention to detail is what makes this prank so sweet (Figure 2).

➡ **Who deserves this?** That coworker who perhaps looks at himself or herself a little too much.

(!) Another suggestion:
Pop out the individual keys on your mark's keyboard, and re-arrange them to spell your name. Next, cover the keyboard in aluminum foil. Using a hobby knife, cut out the section with your name (Figure 3). If needed, use a few of your own keys to complete your name or message.

! Keyboard Signature

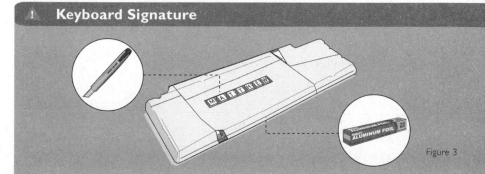

Figure 3

DIFFICULTY LEVEL 4

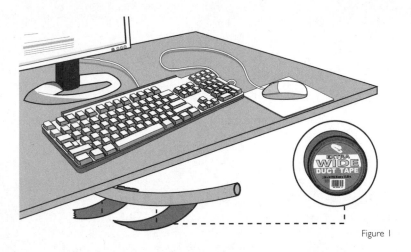

Figure 1

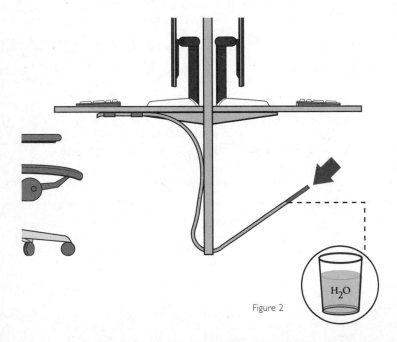

Figure 2

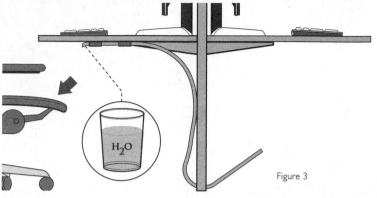

Figure 3

1) **Approximate the length of clear tubing you will need.**
Start by taping the clear tube under your victim's desk, beneath the keyboard area (Figure 1).

2) **Covertly configure the tubing while avoiding detection.**
Hide the tubing as it travels under the cubicle or around the wall. Now, go get a cup of cold water and pour it into the tube on your end. Then wait for your victim to return to his or her desk (Figure 2).

3) **Huff and puff and blow the water through!**
Your target sits down and begins concentrating on work. You grab the end of the tube and quietly blow the water to its new destination (Figure 3). You can hear a sigh from over the wall as your hard-working neighbor feels a cold sensation on his or her lap.

4) **Walk away from the hose before the location and your identity are traced.**
Some of the best pranksters go undetected.

Who deserves this? The coworker with the smallest bladder.

BONUS

Figure 1

1) **Your objective: make it appear that someone was getting sloshed in your mark's office.**
You will need props: a bag of chips, pizza box, empty liquor bottles and/or beer cans.

2) **Safely conceal all the contraband when entering the office.**
It is best not to be caught with empty alcoholic beverages at work.

3) **Fill the trash can with your items.**
Load the wastebasket up with the empty bottles and cans (Figure 1). If you get in early enough the next morning, pour some water around the cans and bottles so they appear to be fresh.

➡ **Who deserves this?** The coworker who is always hung over at work.

OFFICE CABINETS

DIFFICULTY LEVEL I

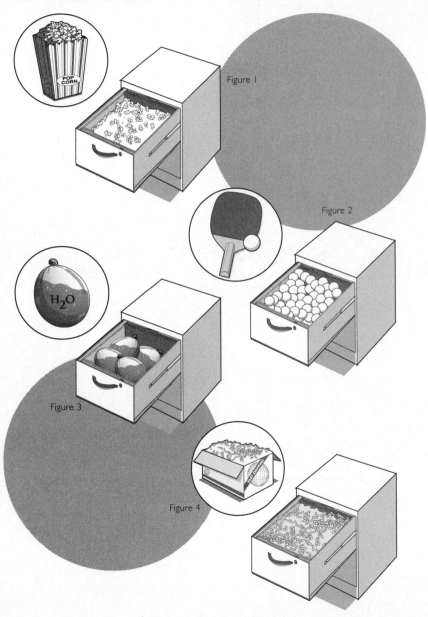

Figure 1

Figure 2

H₂O

Figure 3

Figure 4

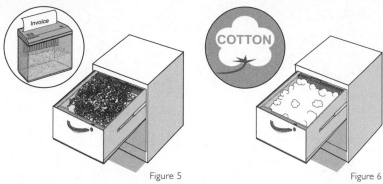

Figure 5 · Figure 6

1) Fill it up!

Drawers are a glutton for punishment. Most of these fillers
are inexpensive bulk purchases or are already available in the
office. Because of the sheer size of some of the packages, you
may want to arrive early or execute this prank after hours to
go undetected.

- **(Figure 1) Yellow carnival popcorn**

- **(Figure 2) Ping-Pong balls**

- **(Figure 3) Water balloons**

- **(Figure 4) Packing peanuts**

- **(Figure 5) Paper shreds**

- **(Figure 6) Cotton**

➡ **Who deserves this?** The coworker who suspects that you
keep a flask in your cabinet.

DIFFICULTY LEVEL 2

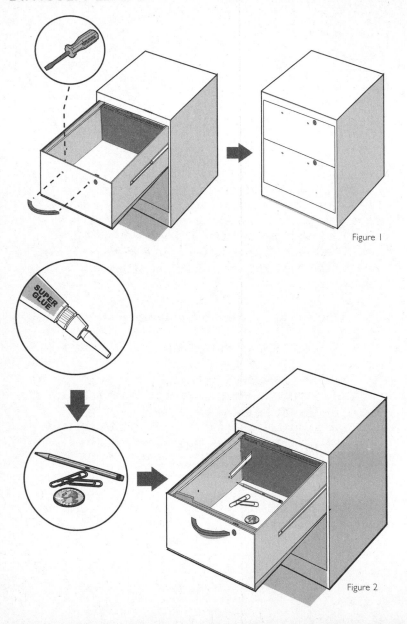

Figure 1

Figure 2

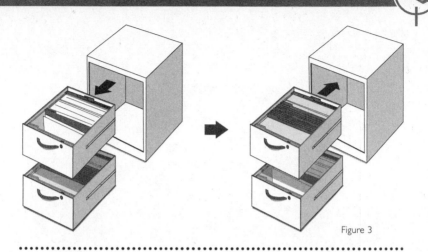

Figure 3

··

1) A few simple tricks to cause drawer confusion.
There are quick and easy tactics to keep your victim
fully alert that he or she is on someone's hit list.

- **Remove all the handles on your mark's
drawers.**
Using a screwdriver, unscrew all the hardware in your
victim's office. Be sure to place the components in a
safe spot for reinstallation (Figure 1).

- **Adhere a few select items randomly on the
bottoms of all the drawers.**
Money, paper clips, and writing utensils work just fine.
Disperse them around in your victim's drawers
(Figure 2).

- **Switch around your victim's drawers.**
Depending on the amount of drawers in your victim's
office, this could get crazy (Figure 3)!

Who deserves this? The coworker who needs a good kick
in the pants, but without the pain.

GELATIN MOLD

DIFFICULTY LEVEL 2

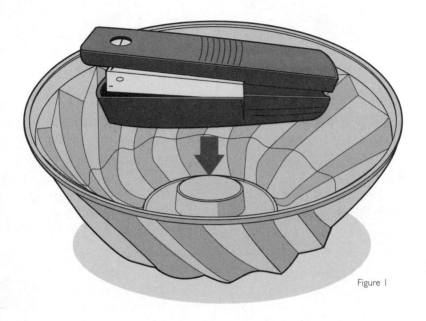

Figure 1

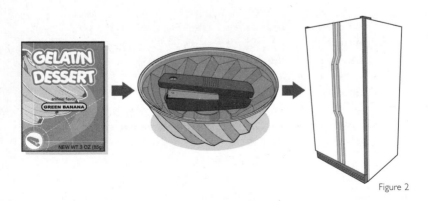

Figure 2

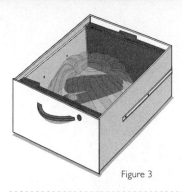

Figure 3

1) Bring a gelatin mold to work, or execute at home the previous night.

Follow the package directions. Bring the water to a boil and remove from heat. Then slowly stir in the powdered gelatin until it's fully dissolved. After that, pour the gelatin water into the mold.

2) Pick your desktop accessory.

You have a few options to choose from: stapler, scissors, calculator, tape, name tag, statue, an award, or pencil sharpener, to list a few (Figure 1).

3) Place your selected accessory into the gelatin mold.

Once you have selected your item, flip it upside down into the mold. Place the mold in the refrigerator, and let it sit for several hours (Figure 2).

4) Check the gelatin for firmness, then place the molded treat back into the mark's desk drawer.

Pick a drawer for your new creation, then gently set down the mold. If it goes unnoticed, drop an anonymous note on his or her desk before it gets messy (Figure 3).

➡ **Who deserves this?** The coworker who doesn't understand your humor.

DIFFICULTY LEVEL 3

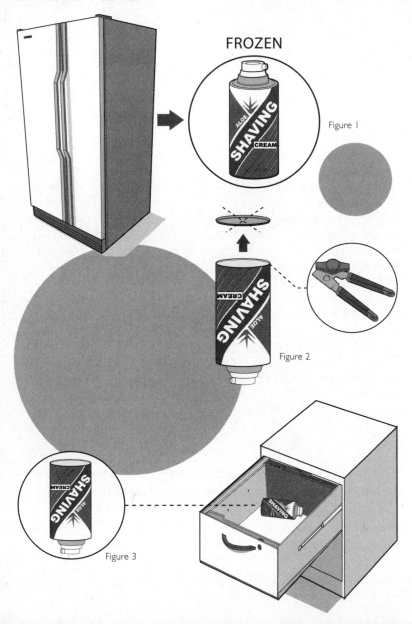

FROZEN

Figure 1

Figure 2

Figure 3

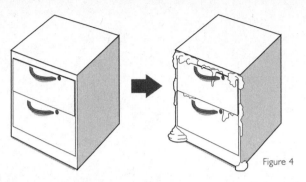

Figure 4

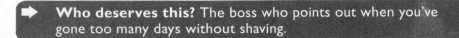

1) Time to make a mess!
Beware; this one is going to leave a mark.

2) Freeze a can of foam shaving cream. Shaving gel will not work.
Once you are satisfied that the can is completely frozen, remove the can from the freezer (Figure 1).

3) Once it is frozen, use a can opener and, slowly cut away the bottom of the can.
If all goes well, the foam should be frozen and the bottom of the can should come off without any problems (Figure 2).

4) Place the newly cut can in your marks empty cabinet.
You probably should empty out his or her cabinet or office drawer first (Figure 3).

5) As the shaving cream defrosts, the foam will expand, filling the cabinet.
A can of shaving cream should fill several cubic feet (Figure 4).

6) This also works great in gym bags, lockers, and wastebaskets with lids.

Who deserves this? The boss who points out when you've gone too many days without shaving.

DIFFICULTY LEVEL 4

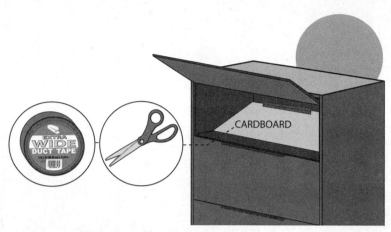

Figure 1

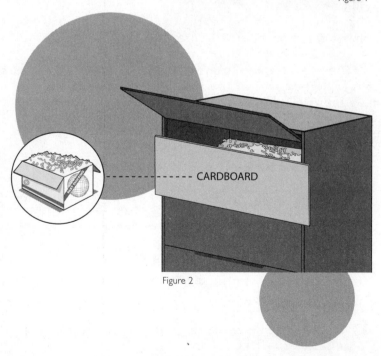

Figure 2

Figure 3

. . . .

1) Prepare the cabinet first by removing all the contents.
Place everything in a cardboard box, and slide it under your desk. It may also be a good idea to post a note in the cabinet in case he or she opens it and really needs something that was in that cabinet when you're out of the office.

2) Create a slant out of cardboard to maximize the avalanche of packing peanuts.
Cut out a piece of cardboard and lean it against the wall, then use tape to hold it into place (Figure 1).

3) Holding a piece of cardboard in front of the cabinet, fill up the compartment.
Once completed, shut the door, and then slide out the cardboard. Clean up any peanuts that may have fallen on the floor. This step might take two individuals (Figure 2).

4) Be patient; it could happen anytime.
If you are unsure when it's going to happen, set up a web cam for surveillance. I can guarantee you'll know when your victim springs the trap; the sound of disgust will fill the office (Figure 3).

➡ **Who deserves this?** Anyone who actually still files.

CRICKET DRAWERS

DIFFICULTY LEVEL 4

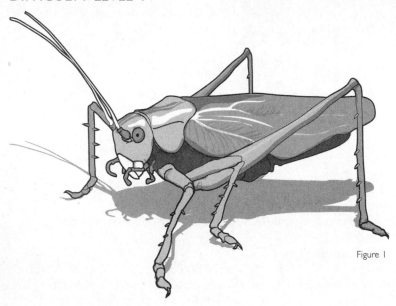

Figure 1

Cricket x 50

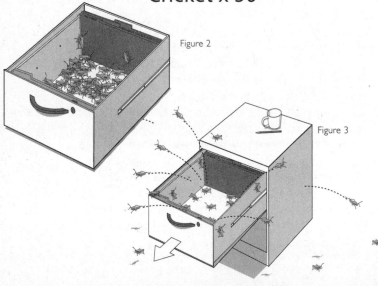

Figure 2

Figure 3

1) Crickets: food for some, annoying for others.
You can bulk order crickets for pet food (Figure 1). Depending on the space, you can order batches of 100 up to 1000. Just remember that crickets are hard as hell to catch, and you might be forced to help round them up.

2) Place the cricket colony in a well-sealed drawer.
Find a drawer with a controllable environment, one that will keep the crickets contained when closed. You would hate to have the crickets run amok in a huge 20-drawer filing cabinet (Figure 2).

3) The next time your mark looks for the T.P.S. reports, he or she will be shocked!
If the crickets survived, they will be more than happy to free themselves from their cabinet holding cell (Figure 3).

➡ **Who deserves this?** Better question—who can handle this?

(!) Another suggestion:
First, purchase a fake rodent. Then tie the rodent to a small piece of clear fishing line. Fasten the other end of the fishing line to the cabinet door (Figure 4). If all goes well, the door will open up, and it will appear the rodent is attempting to jump out.

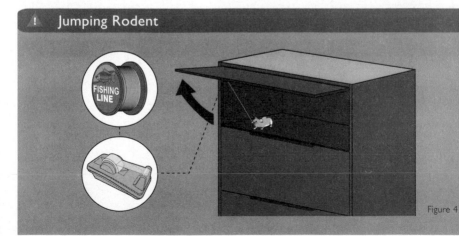

! Jumping Rodent

Figure 4

BONUS

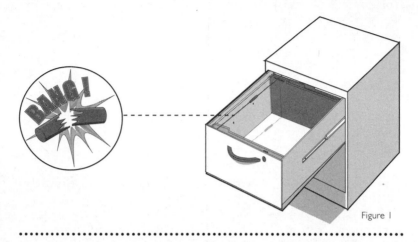

Figure 1

1) **Pull-string firecrackers are a very simple type of firework, creating an unexpected bang!**
Plus, they are dirt cheap and relatively safe if not abused.

2) **Cabinet drawer with report.**
Tie or tape one end of the string on the drawer, and tie the other end to the cabinet housing (Figure 1). Your mark will pull out the drawer, only to be startled by an unanticipated bang!

Who deserves this? The coworker who is easily startled.

OFFICE ENTRANCE  4

PAPER HOLE DOOR

DIFFICULTY LEVEL 1

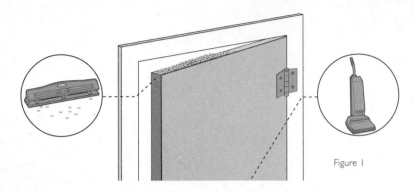

Figure 1

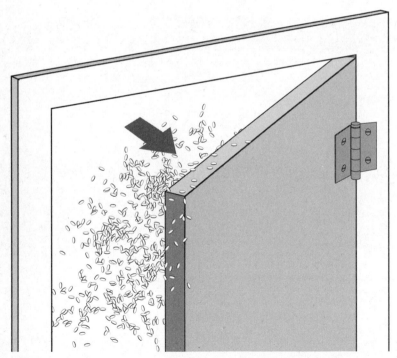

Figure 2

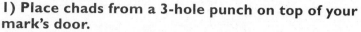

1) Place chads from a 3-hole punch on top of your mark's door.
If you feel your pile isn't significant enough, just punch out some more (Figure 1).

2) Vacuum up any chads that might have fallen while you were placing the pile on top of the door.
Don't have a vacuum? Then hand-pick them up, or your target may notice the trap before it is sprung.

3) Raining chads!
With a slight push of the door, chads will fall down in full force. Almost lighter then air, they will certainly hit their mark. Some of them will seek out your mark's hair; others might try to penetrate your victim's mouth. Whatever their motive may be, they will definitely leave a mess (Figure 2).

➡ **Who deserves this?** Anyone you think deserves a warning on who not to mess with.

(!) Another suggestion:
Does your coworker have a ceiling fan? If so, fill the blades with chads. With a flip of the switch your victim will instantly have a very messy office (Figure 3).

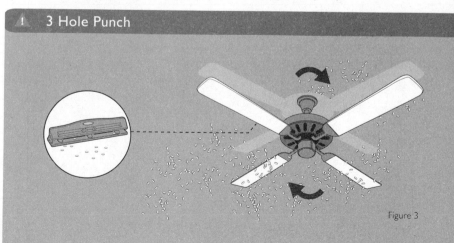

! 3 Hole Punch

Figure 3

DIFFICULTY LEVEL 2

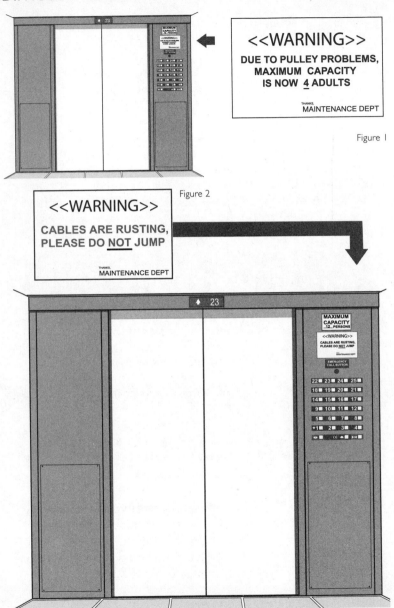

<<WARNING>>

DUE TO PULLEY PROBLEMS,
MAXIMUM CAPACITY
IS NOW 4 ADULTS

THANKS,
MAINTENANCE DEPT

Figure 1

Figure 2

<<WARNING>>

CABLES ARE RUSTING,
PLEASE DO NOT JUMP

THANKS,
MAINTENANCE DEPT

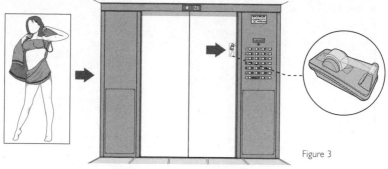

Figure 3

---

1) Create a fraudulent sign warning elevator riders of potential problems.

Before pulling this prank off, take note of any corporate or maintenance signs around the building. You will want to mimic the signs to the best of your ability for authenticity. Using your computer skills, recreate one of the signs with a bogus message, then place it above the keypad in the elevator. Elevator phobia or not, people will still take note of your message with some degree of concern.

- **Due to pulley problems, maximum capacity is now four adults.**
  Ride the elevator a few times, and see if anyone really decides to step off (Figure 1).

- **What happens if we jump—do we die?**
  Post the note, then ride the elevator a few times, and randomly jump and smile (Figure 2).

- **Obscene image revealed; everyone look away.**
  When no one else is in the elevator, securely tape a provocative image right on the edge of the door. When the door shuts, everyone will be shocked to see what has been revealed (Figure 3).

 Who deserves this? Anyone with a phobia about getting stuck in an elevator.

DIFFICULTY LEVEL 3

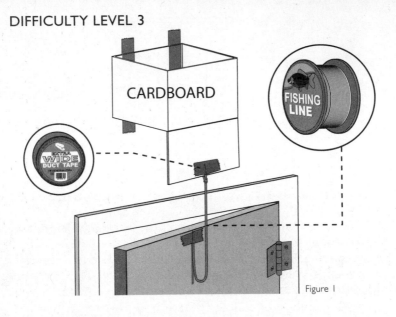

Figure 1

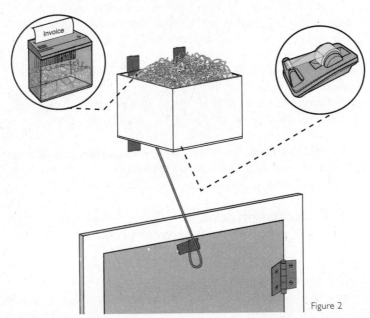

Figure 2

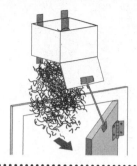

Figure 3

1) Prepare a small cardboard box to hold your paper shreds.

Using a utility knife, remove three sides of the bottom of the box so it can swing open.

2) Install the cardboard box above your mark's doorway.

Use tape to fasten it against the wall. The flap should open away from the wall (Figure 1).

3) Attach string to the door and the box bottom.

Before doing this, you will want to close the door and the box to measure the exact amount of string that is needed (Figure 1).

4) Close the bottom of the box, and lightly tape it shut.

It is important not to tape too much, because you will want the bottom to swing out when tugged.

5) Fill the box with paper shreds.

There is a very good chance this whole rigging could come down when the door opens, so use filler that won't cause harm (Figure 2).

6) Wait for your victim to enter.

Once he or she opens the door, the bottom of the box will swing open, spilling all its contents (Figure 3).

➡ **Who deserves this?** Anyone who is less stressed at work than you.

DIFFICULTY LEVEL 4

Figure 1

Figure 2

1) Using a hammer and screwdriver, remove the pins from the hinges.
Once you have finished, the door should balance on the hardware (Figure 1).

2) Help your victim start off the morning the right way, with a falling door.
Your mark will attempt to push the door open, only to see it crash down to the floor! You may want to clear the area behind the door to avoid damage (Figure 2). Be cautious—your intended victim or innocent bystanders could possibly get hurt while the door is falling.

➡ **Who deserves this?** That busybody downstairs who doesn't understand that a closed door means "Don't come in."

(!) Another suggestion:
Two more quick and easy door pranks. The first one: unscrew the hardware and completely remove it (Figure 3). The second: place some petroleum jelly under the knob (Figure 4).

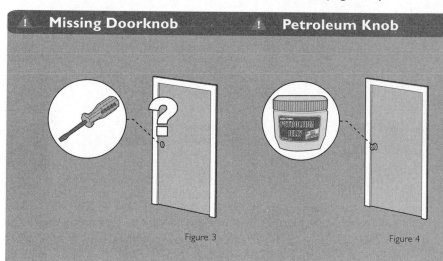

! **Missing Doorknob**   ! **Petroleum Knob**

Figure 3

Figure 4

DIFFICULTY LEVEL 5

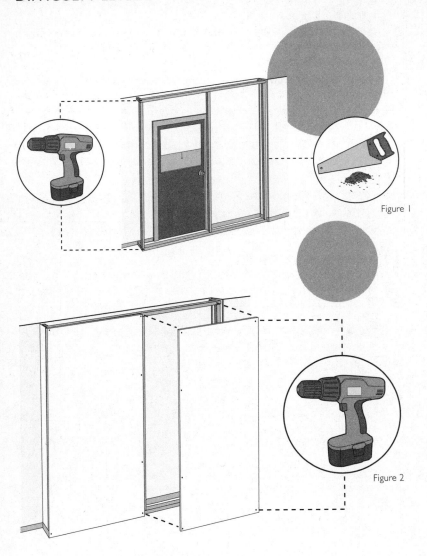

Figure 1

Figure 2

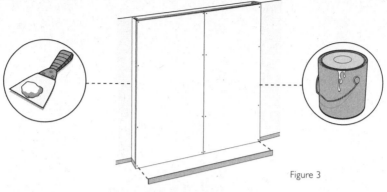

Figure 3

1) Build a freestanding frame around the door. Try to integrate it into the existing wall.
You can pre-cut the lumber at home if you wish to speed up the build at your office. Build the frame freestanding, and see if it is possible to wedge the frame between the ceiling and the floor. If not, then use one or two screws into the wall to hold it into place (Figure 1).

2) Add a drywall surface.
Because this wall is only temporary, the thinnest drywall available is recommended. Using a drill, screw the drywall over the newly constructed frame (Figure 2).

3) Spackle the corners, and add drywall screws.
Using plaster and a putty knife, spackle all your screw heads, and clean up the drywall seams. Once they are dry, lightly sand off any extra plaster, and prepare the surface for paint (Figure 3).

4) Your final step is matching the paint and adding a baseboard if needed.
After you paint the wall, match the baseboard for a professional look.

 Who deserves this? Someone who really did something extremely awful to deserve this much time and dedication.

DOORBELL DRENCH

DIFFICULTY LEVEL 5

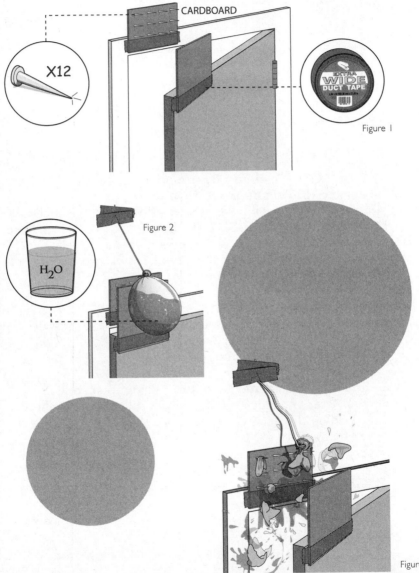

CARDBOARD

X12

Figure 1

H_2O

Figure 2

Figure 3

1) Tape a small piece of cardboard onto the door frame with several sharp tacks sticking out.
Tacks or nails will work; just make sure the sharp points are exposed (Figure 1).

2) Cut out a small piece of cardboard and attach it to the door, using tape.
This will protect the water balloon when the door is shut. This piece should be only as big as the cardboard with the tacks. The higher the piece, the farther the door will have to open (Figure 1).

3) Position a water balloon above the cardboard.
Using string, securely tape or tie the end to the wall so it will hold a fully filled water balloon (Figure 2).

4) The next time your victim enters the office, he'll be surprised to feel a watery welcome.
The balloon will flip over the cardboard and explode on impact (Figure 3). This prank works only with an office door that opens inward.

➡ **Who deserves this?** The coworker who never knocks before entering.

(!) Another suggestion:
A simpler execution would be attaching a non-water balloon to the back of the door and placing a tack on the frame or wall (Figure 4). When your mark enters the office, she will be greeted with a bang!

⚠ Balloon Bell

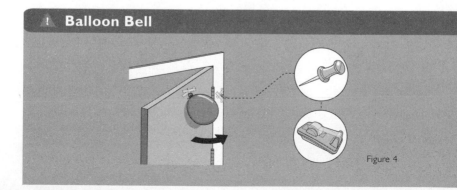

Figure 4

BONUS

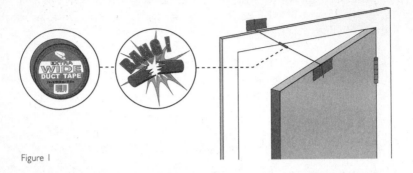

Figure 1

1) Tape or tie a pull-string firecracker to your victim's door and doorframe.
You have a few placement options: high and out of sight, or eye level—your choice.

2) Catch him off guard!
Your victim will come strolling into the office only to be flabbergasted by a simple 5-cent bang (Figure 1).

➡ **Who deserves this?** Anyone who springs the trap.

COMPUTER ABUSE 5

DIFFICULTY LEVEL 1

Figure 1

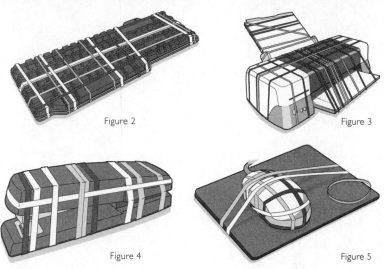

Figure 2

Figure 3

Figure 4

Figure 5

1) Attack of the Rubber Band Man.

Seize a large bag of rubber bands from the supply closet. Intertwine them around the flat panel monitor until it begins to resemble a plaid flannel shirt (Figure 1).

➡ **Who deserves this?** Anyone you consider harmless but worthy of pranking.

(!) Four more quick suggestions:

Take your skillful craft and execute the same handiwork on the keyboard, mouse, printer, stapler, fax machine, pencil sharpener, and picture frames (Figures 2–5).

DIFFICULTY LEVEL I

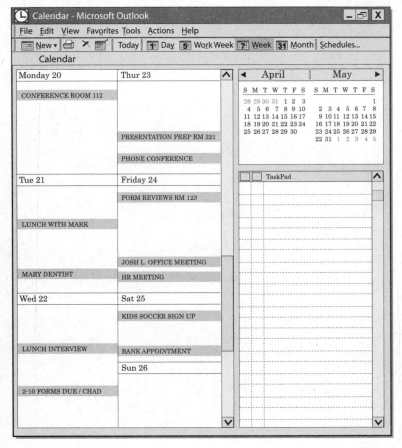

Figure I

1) Gain access to your coworker's computer during work hours.
This will take only a few minutes, so keep an eye on your victim and wait for the appropriate time to infiltrate his personal computer.

2) Alter your victim's calendar by inserting random appointments.
Locate the calendar and begin to come up with bogus commitments. Most of the appointments you conjure up will be very dificult for your mark to verify, so he will be forced to authenticate them before deleting (Figure 1).

3) Family appointments work just as well as company appointments.
Knowing family names will help. Soccer sign-up, dentist appointments, and family engagements will really confuse your victim.

➡ **Who deserves this?** A coworker who is never quite busy enough.

(!) Another suggestion:
If you arrive early, type in a bogus password on your mark's computer a few times until it locks you out (Figure 2).

! Password Lockout

Employee Login	☒
Login	
Login name:	JBOYCE
Password:	*****
Domain	
OK CANCEL HELP	

Figure 2

A S D F G   X3

AUTOCORRECT

DIFFICULTY LEVEL 2

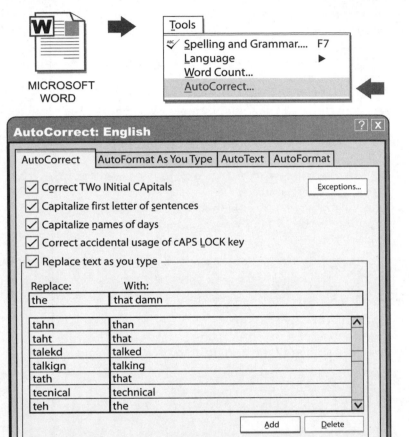

MICROSOFT WORD

Tools

ᴬᴮᶜ✓ Spelling and Grammar....	F7
Language	▶
Word Count...	
AutoCorrect...	

AutoCorrect: English [?] [X]

| AutoCorrect | AutoFormat As You Type | AutoText | AutoFormat |

☑ Correct TWo INitial CApitals   Exceptions...

☑ Capitalize first letter of sentences

☑ Capitalize names of days

☑ Correct accidental usage of cAPS LOCK key

☑ Replace text as you type

Replace:	With:
the	that damn

tahn	than
taht	that
talekd	talked
talkign	talking
tath	that
tecnical	technical
teh	the

Add   Delete

☑ Automatically use suggestions from the spelling checker

OK   CLOSE

Figure 1

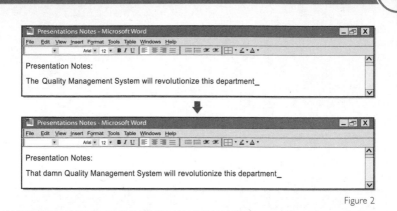

Figure 2

1) AutoCorrect can do more than correct misspelling and mistyping.
It can also be manipulated to change correctly spelled words into something totally random.

2) Go into Microsoft Word and select the Tools menu.
Under Tools, select AutoCorrect for the dialog box (Figure 1).

3) Modify existing entries and replace them with new words.
Pick a common word often used. We will use the word *the* for our example. Replace the word *the* with *that damn*.

4) Let the typing begin, and your newly added words will appear.
Whenever your victim types *the,* it's automatically corrected to *that damn.* Your mark might not notice it, depending on how fast he or she types (Figure 2).

5) Be sure to keep a list of words you switch, so you can easily fix them.

➡ **Who deserves this?** The coworker who constantly corrects your grammar.

DIFFICULTY LEVEL 2

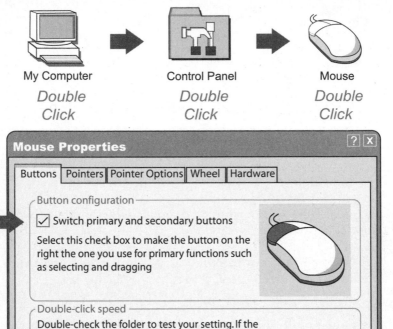

My Computer	Control Panel	Mouse
Double Click	*Double Click*	*Double Click*

Mouse Properties   [?] [X]

| Buttons | Pointers | Pointer Options | Wheel | Hardware |

Button configuration

☑ Switch primary and secondary buttons

Select this check box to make the button on the right the one you use for primary functions such as selecting and dragging

Double-click speed

Double-check the folder to test your setting. If the folder does not open or close, try using a slower setting.

Speed: Slow ——————⏷—————— Fast

ClickLock

☐ Turn on ClickLock   [Settings....]

Enables you to highlight or drag without holding down the mouse button. To set, briefly press the mouse button. To release, click the mouse button again.

[OK]   [Cancel]   [Apply]

Figure 1

126   CHAPTER **5**: COMPUTER ABUSE

1) Switch the primary and secondary buttons on your victim's mouse.

Double-click on *My Computer*, then double-click on *Control Panel*. Locate your mouse controls, then double-click on the icon. Locate the button configuration, then select the *Switch primary and secondary buttons* (Figure 1).

Who deserves this? The coworker who never seems to have issues with his or her computer.

(!) Four more quick suggestions:

There are several other ways to disable a computer mouse. Liquid Paper the optical, tape over the optical, glue the mouse to the mouse pad, and, of course, unplug the USB behind the computer (Figures 2–5).

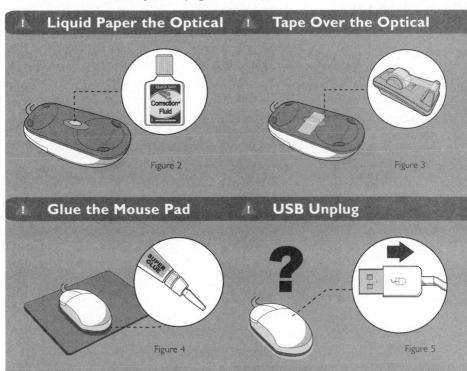

! Liquid Paper the Optical

Figure 2

! Tape Over the Optical

Figure 3

! Glue the Mouse Pad

Figure 4

! USB Unplug

Figure 5

DIFFICULTY LEVEL 3

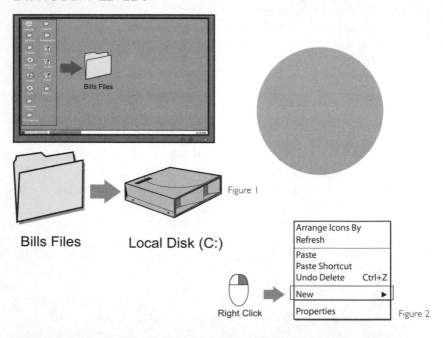

Figure 1

Bills Files   Local Disk (C:)

Arrange Icons By	
Refresh	
Paste	
Paste Shortcut	
Undo Delete	Ctrl+Z
New	▶
Properties	

Right Click

Figure 2

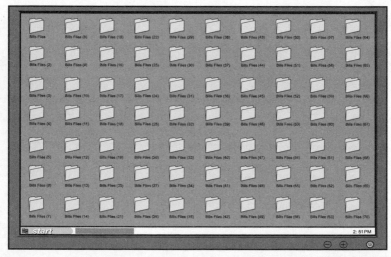

Figure 3

Figure 4

• •

1) Which folder will your corporate contestant select?

This isn't a game of skill, just a game filled with frustration and irritation.

2) Create a new folder on your victim's desktop, then drag all your victim's icons into that folder.

Right-click on the mouse, then select *New Folder* from the menu. Label that folder *Desktop Files* for future reference. Next, drag all your victim's icons into the new *Desktop Files* folder. DO NOT DELETE; instead, move the folder onto your victim's C: drive for safe keeping (Figure 1).

3) Next, create a new folder, and duplicate the folder until it fills up your mark's screen.

Create a new folder labeled _(mark's name)_ files (Figure 2). Then copy and paste that folder until you have the entire screen filled with almost the identical folder (Figure 3).

4) Time to play the game!

Post a note on the contestant's screen outlining the game rules (Figure 4). The files are so important that your mark will be forced to search every folder, only to discover the material is still missing.

 Who deserves this? The coworker who gloats about his or her time management skills.

DIFFICULTY LEVEL 3

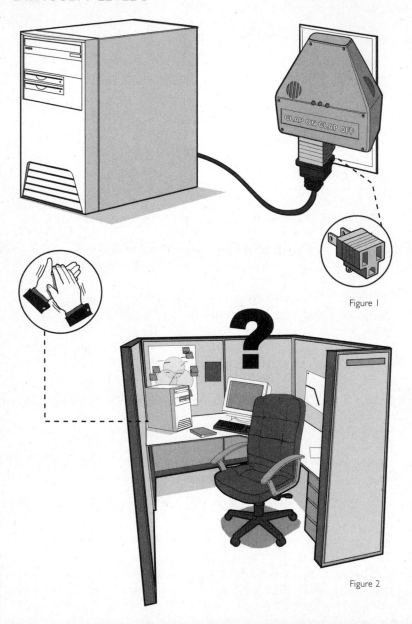

Figure 1

Figure 2

1) AS SEEN ON TV!
Purchase one of those ingenious clapping devices that is activated by a sound sensing component.

2) Attach an electrical plug adapter to your mark's computer cord.
You may have to convert his or her 3-prong computer cable to fit the 2-prong clapper-device outlet (Figure 1).

3) Time for a few unsuspecting computer shutdowns.
With a simple clap, you will have the power any time to shut down his or her PC. The device might also pick up other office noises; you can adjust the sensitivity dial to increase or decrease the device's sensitivity (Figure 2). Just remember that work will be lost.

Who deserves this? The loudest person in the office.

(!) Another suggestion:
Conceal a portable radio in your victim's office with the clapper device plugged into it. Now, switch the radio on, then clap to turn it off. Once it is off, increase the volume. The next time the device is activated by sound sensing, the deafening sound will knock your victim off his or her chair (Figure 3).

! Hidden Noise

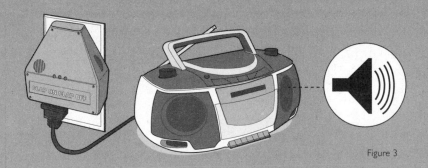

CLAP ON CLAP OFF

Figure 3

DIFFICULTY LEVEL 3

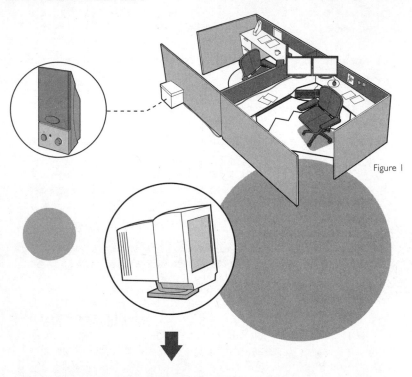

Figure 1

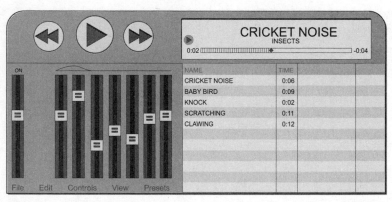

Figure 2

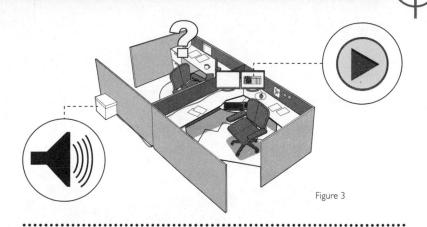

Figure 3

· ·

1) A quiet office can almost drive someone clinically insane.

But as soon as a faint sound infringes on their personal space, they call out the watchdogs. Their immediate response is, where is that music coming from?

2) Run speaker wire to a obscure location in your the office.

Conceal the speaker in a planter, file box, or cored-out book—you get the idea (Figure 1).

3) Prepare a diabolical playlist.

Jam-pack your playlist with cats, crickets, knocking, scratching—anything you feel will turn a few heads (Figure 2).

4) Cautiously play the sounds.

Never press Play when someone is on top of the speaker, because your fun will be short lived (Figure 3).

5) Hells Bells!

Go for the gusto, wait for your mark to be on the phone, and play AC/DC's "Hells Bells" at Level 11!

➡ **Who deserves this?** The chick down the hall who doesn't appreciate Heavy Metal Tuesdays.

DIFFICULTY LEVEL 3

Figure 1

Figure 2

1) Basic computer skills are a must at work!

Computer skills are mandatory in any office. The first step to using the computer is the keyboard. This trick is intended for those who still peek at the keys while typing.

2) Which color is your victim's keyboard?

Depending on the keyboard, you have two options. If the keyboard is black, use a permanent marker and delete all the white text (Figure 1). If it's white, Liquid Paper works great (Figure 2). Beware—the keyboard could be destroyed after this stunt.

Who deserves this? Anyone who needs a laugh and actually has a sense of humor to appreciate a good joke.

(!) Added bonus:

Another great keyboard trick is quickly switching keys to spell words. Combine this with the Textless Keyboard and black out all the letters except for your victim's name or your name in the middle of the keyboard (Figures 3–8).

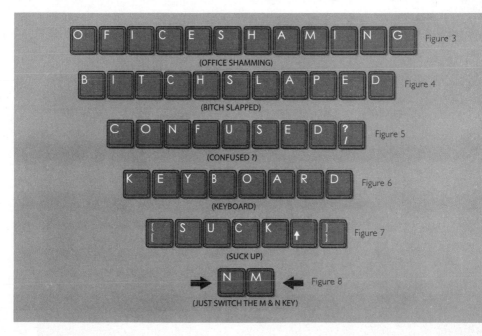

Figure 3

(OFFICE SHAMMING)

Figure 4

(BITCH SLAPPED)

Figure 5

(CONFUSED ?)

Figure 6

(KEYBOARD)

Figure 7

(SUCK UP)

Figure 8

(JUST SWITCH THE M & N KEY)

DIFFICULTY LEVEL 4

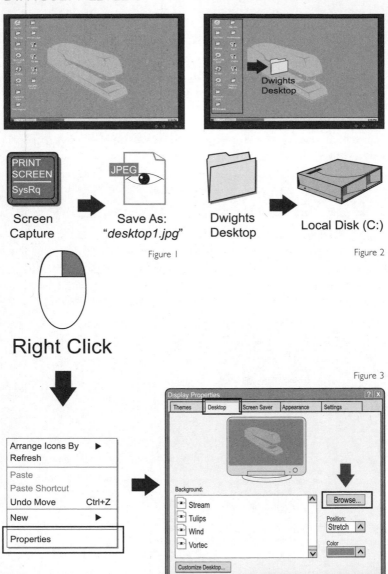

Screen
Capture

Save As:
"*desktop1.jpg*"

Figure 1

Dwights
Desktop

Local Disk (C:)

Figure 2

Figure 3

Right Click

Arrange Icons By ▶
Refresh
Paste
Paste Shortcut
Undo Move   Ctrl+Z
New   ▶
Properties

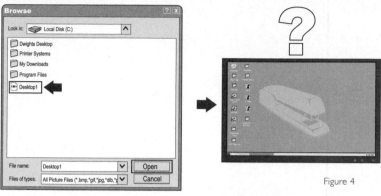

Figure 4

1) Locate the *Print Screen* command and execute.

Locate the *Print Screen* command and execute. This tool will take a snapshot of your victim's current desktop. The computer then saves the image to the *Clipboard*. Your next step is to paste the image into a program that will allow you to save it as a jpeg, then save it on to the C: drive (Figure 1).

2) Hide all the icons and folders on the C: drive.

Clean off the entire desktop and place all the files and icons in a new folder, which will then be placed on the C: drive (Figure 2). At this point, nothing should be on the desktop.

3) Locate your Print Screen file and create the custom wallpaper which will resemble the original desktop.

Right-click on the mouse and select *Properties*. Next, go to the *Desktop* and select *Browse* (Figure 3). You are now attempting to locate the earlier image you created when you hit *Print Screen*. Once you've found it, select the file and press *Open* (Figure 4). If everything works as planned, your victim's computer should look as if it has a full screen of icons and folders. As soon as your victim starts clicking on the wallpaper image, it will appear that the computer has locked up again!

Who deserves this? Someone who is somewhat computer illiterate.

DIFFICULTY LEVEL 5

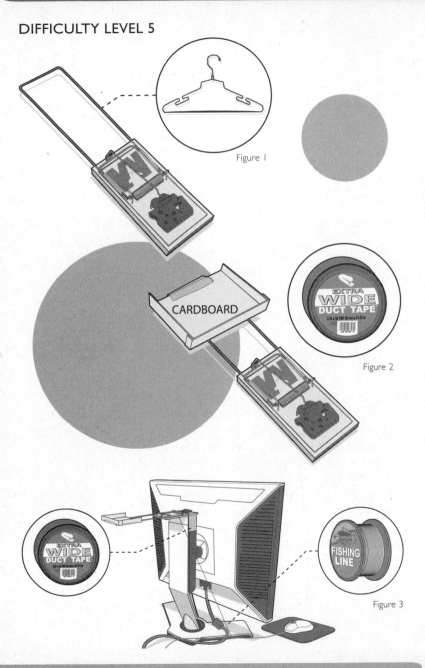

Figure 1

CARDBOARD

Figure 2

Figure 3

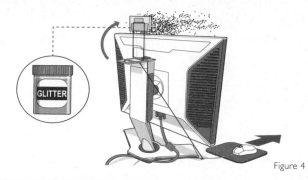

Figure 4

....

1) Cut a metal coat hanger, and bend it into shape.
Depending on the make and model of the monitor, the
length of the wire will need to be cut accordingly. Once the
wire is cut, bend it into shape and tape it onto the spring-
loaded bar (Figure 1).

**2) Use cardboard to construct the launching plat-
form for the glitter.**
Once the device is assembled, tape the box to the spring-
loaded bar (Figure 2).

**3) Fasten the mousetrap to the back of the monitor,
and then tie the fishing lines in place.**
Try to keep it out of view. This could be tricky and may
not work in all offices. Before setting the trap, tie one end
of the fishing line to the mousetrap lever, and then fix the
other end to the mouse cable. It is important to move the
mouse out of place, so your victim will reposition it once he
or she sits down. Then set the mousetrap (Figure 3).

**4) Delicately pour a few tablespoons of glitter onto
the cardboard launch pad.**
Try not to set off the trap when pouring the glitter. If all
goes well, the trap should spring once your mark moves the
mouse back to its original location (Figure 4).

(!) Use caution; glitter could damage someone's eyes.

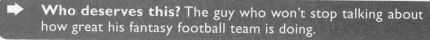

Who deserves this? The guy who won't stop talking about
how great his fantasy football team is doing.

BROKEN KEYBOARD

DIFFICULTY LEVEL 5

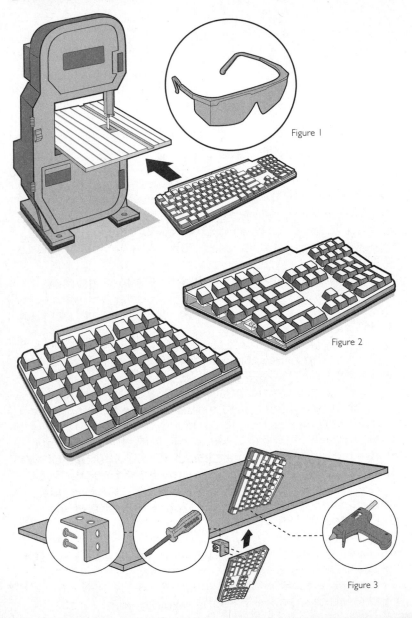

Figure 1

Figure 2

Figure 3

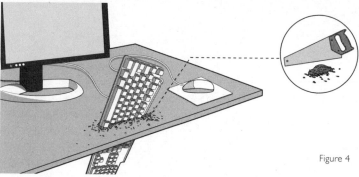

Figure 4

....

1) Contact the IT department to acquire a broken keyboard.
Instead of amputating your office mate's keyboard, contact the friendly people in the IT department and see if they have any broken models that are similar.

2) Cut a diagonal line, following the key configuration on the keyboard.
Wearing safety glasses, slowly run the keyboard through a band saw at a slight angle, so the cut matches up with the key configuration. You may have to execute this at a workshop (Figures 1 and 2).

3) Use hardware to screw the keyboard to the bottom of the table.
Locate a small "L" bracket and screw it to the back of the keyboard. Next, screw the "L" bracket to the bottom of the table. Make sure the screws don't reach the table surface, because the desk will be ruined. Use a low-heat hot glue gun or sticky wax for the section of keyboard on top of the table (Figure 3).

4) Add sawdust around the keyboard to cover up the keyboard edges.
This will give the illusion that the keyboard is impaled in the office table as a result of cubicle rage (Figure 4).

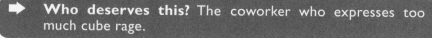

Who deserves this? The coworker who expresses too much cube rage.

BONUS

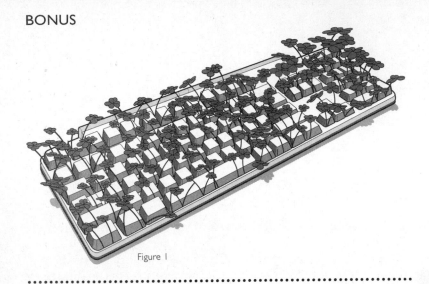

Figure I

1) Prior to entering the office, round up a large amount of clovers, dandelions, or blades of grass.
Place the vegetation in a paper or plastic bag for easy transport.

2) Start placing each individual plant between the keys.
This step will take painstaking determination and time, but it's worth it. Fill the keyboard up as much as possible (Figure I).

Who deserves this? Anyone who seems to have a lot of extra time.

(!) Another suggestion:
When placing the blades of grass between the keys, use super glue to insure they stay. Your victim will be forced to cut down the grass in order to use the keyboard.

ELECTRONIC EQUIPMENT —6

DIFFICULTY LEVEL 1

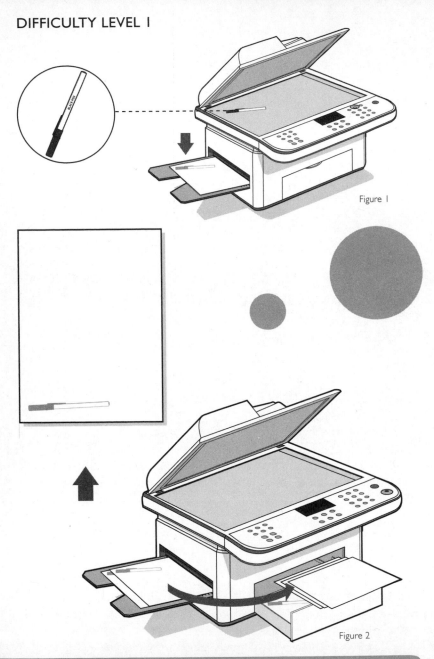

Figure 1

Figure 2

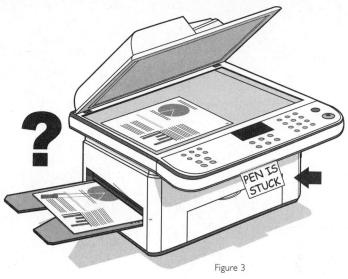

Figure 3

1) **Someone's "pen-is" stuck?**
Quick and easy, this is a fun way to trick your fellow employees.

2) **Create several copies of an ordinary ballpoint pen.**
Perform this step undetected (Figure 1).

3) **Randomly place the newly printed pages back into the paper drawer.**
How you return them is your decision. You can shuffle them among the clean white sheets, or stack the newly created copies right on top of the stack of paper (Figure 2).

4) **Create a sign alarming your fellow associates that a problem has materialized.**
This semi-vulgar sign will definitely catch the attention of a few perverted individuals you work with. They'll be surprised to see it wasn't just a raunchy joke when defaced copies start to slide out of the machine (Figure 3).

 Who deserves this? An unsuspecting victim who was counting on those printouts for a meeting in 5 minutes.

DIFFICULTY LEVEL I

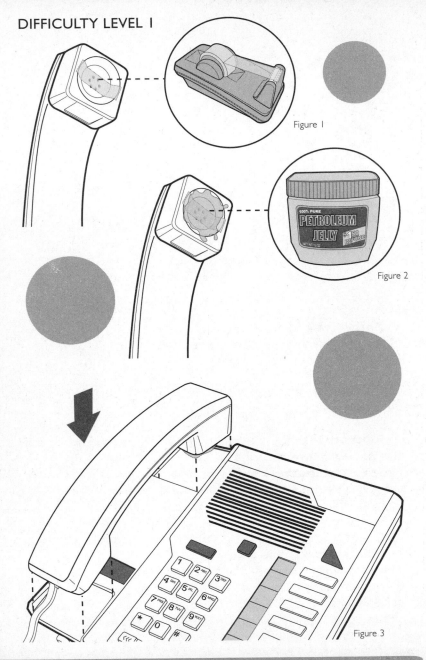

Figure I

Figure 2

Figure 3

1) Everyone loves petroleum jelly—right?

Believe it or not, people don't necessary like petroleum jelly in their ears. On the way to work, stop by your local grocery or drug store and pick up a small container of this mysterious lubricant jelly. Try to keep it concealed when entering your place of employment. This magical jelly may raise a few eyebrows if seen.

2) Tape the speaker vents to protect the phone's innards.

Lay a small piece of clear tape over the earpiece before applying the jelly. This will keep the phone in good working condition after the fun is over (Figure 1).

3) Apply jelly to the earpiece.

Now apply the petroleum jelly over the tape on the earpiece (Figure 2). Next, place the phone back on the receiver (Figure 3). At this point you have two options: call your victim, or wait until someone important calls to discuss business. The second option could be most rewarding, but there is a chance of being reprimanded if it's a client or the boss.

Who deserves this? The guy who needs to clean his ears, because it's starting to become a distraction.

(!) Two quick suggestions:

A few more suggestions while messing with your coworkers phone: Lightly super glue the phone to the receiver (Figure 4). When your victim goes to grab the phone, he or she'll be shocked to see everything fly up! Velcro has the same effect but doesn't destroy the phone (Figure 5).

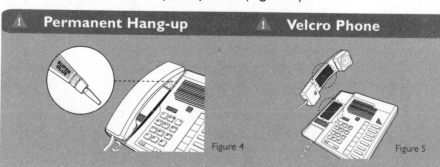

Permanent Hang-up   **Velcro Phone**

Figure 4

Figure 5

DIFFICULTY LEVEL 2

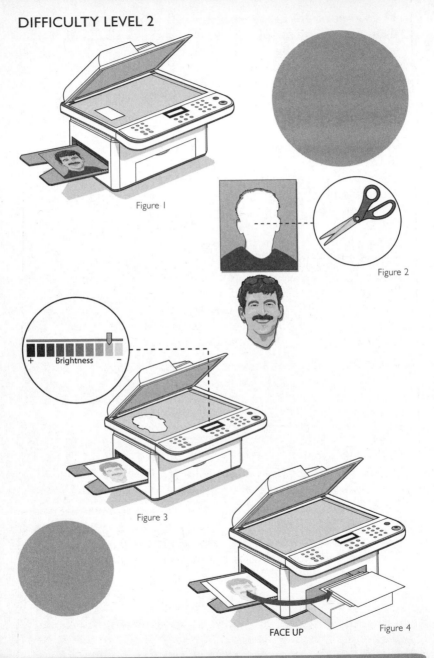

Figure 1

Figure 2

Figure 3

FACE UP   Figure 4

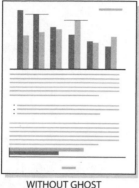
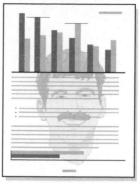

WITHOUT GHOST WITH GHOST

Figure 5

1) Enlarge a photo of your victim.
Using the photocopier, increase the size of one of the many personal photos on your victim's desk (Figure 1).

2) On the newly enlarged printout, cut out the background image.
Because you are going to recreate this image, you don't want the background to show up, just your victim's head (Figure 2).

3) Locate the brightness controls on the copier, and lower the saturation.
Once you've lowered it, begin to produce several copies of only your victim's head. The printouts should be very light, almost ghostly (Figure 3).

4) Place the newly created pages back into the copy drawer.
Place them face up, so when they come out of the machine again, your victim's image is barely visible on the front (Figure 4).

5) Now, let's see if anyone notices.
If all goes well, your victim's ghost will appear on the front of several unsuspecting presentations (Figure 5).

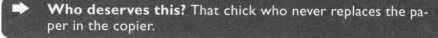

Who deserves this? That chick who never replaces the paper in the copier.

MASS CALL FORWARDING

DIFFICULTY LEVEL 2

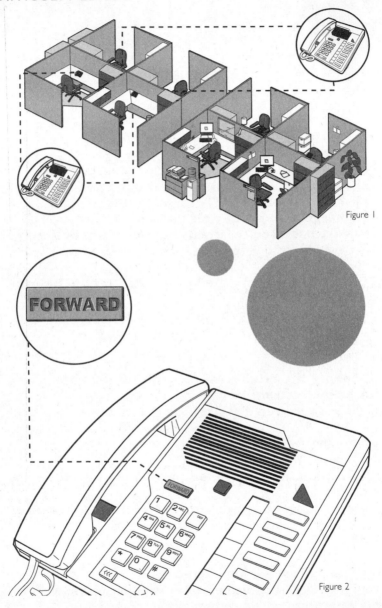

Figure 1

FORWARD

Figure 2

1) Just had a corporate restructure? Perfect!
That should mean you have a few vacant offices in your
building (Figure 1).

**2) Locate all the telephones not in use, and forward
all those calls to your victim's phone.**
Locate the Call Forward button on the unit. Next, follow
the instructions and insert your victim's number (Figure 2).
The phone in your office is probably identical, so review the
steps before venturing off.

**3) Most outside callers will be unaware of the layoffs
and will continue to call the empty offices.**
Your victim will start receive a large number of random
calls, most of which will be asking for former employees
(Figure 3). He or she will have to spend the next few days
locating the rogue phones and undoing your shenanigans.

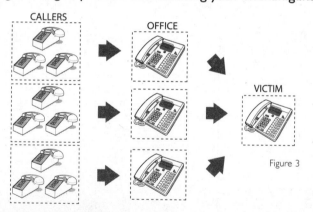

Figure 3

➡ **Who deserves this?** The phone desk person who is prone
to mess up transfers.

(!) Another suggestion:
If you're traveling for business with your mark, schedule a
ridiculous wake-up call for him or her.

DIFFICULTY LEVEL 2

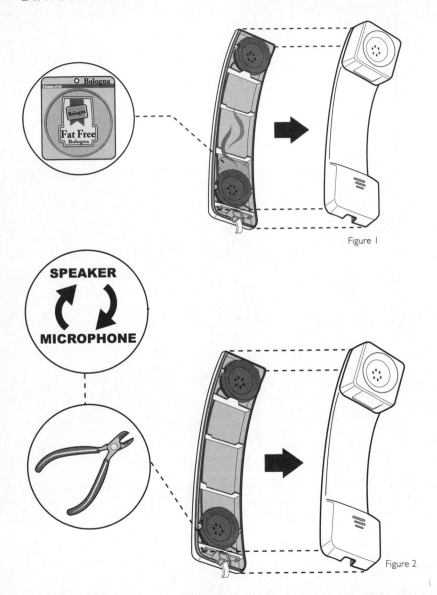

Figure 1

SPEAKER

MICROPHONE

Figure 2

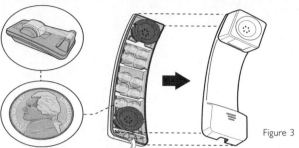

Figure 3

1) Attack your victim's phone with multiple technical problems.

You have several options on how disrupt your mark's communication. The phone will need to be disassembled by snapping the two halves apart. Depending on the make or model of the phone, these pranks might not work. Most likely, your phone is the same model as your victim's, so practice disassembling yours first.

- **Smells like a bad phone call!**
Disassemble the receiver, place strips of bologna in the housing, and reassemble (Figure 1).

- **Switch the speaker with the microphone.**
Locate the two wires responsible for the speaker and microphone inside the phone. Next, using wire cutters, cut the wires. Now switch the wires, and reattach them. Caution—you may want to unplug the phone to avoid a short circuit (Figure 2).

- **Using coins, weight down your victim's phone over a long period of time.**
Gradually tape coins in your victim's phone. Once you've slowly filled up your victim's phone over a few weeks, let him get comfortable with the weight. Now, remove the coins and watch your mark misjudge the weight of the phone, causing a head collision (Figure 3).

Who deserves this? That coworker who is so loud on the phone you can't help but listen to the conversation.

DIFFICULTY LEVEL 3

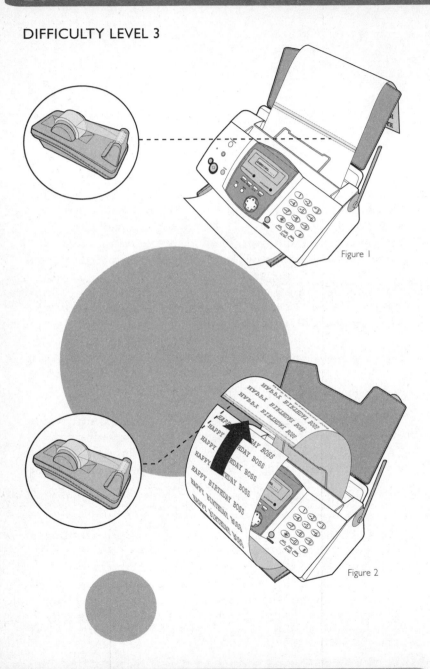

Figure 1

Figure 2

1) Begin by taping 2 or 3 sheets together, depending on the fax machine.
Loop and tape sheets around the fax machine to form an endless sheet of paper (Figure 1).

2) Now type in your victim's fax number, and hit the _SEND_ button.
If this is done right, the paper should continually run through the machine.

3) The next day, your victim will come to work with a paperless fax machine.
The fax will keep running until your victim's machine runs out of paper or ink (Figure 2). This prank will work on most fax machines, but not all.

➡ **Who deserves this?** Some fool who hasn't heard of e-mail.

(!) Two quick suggestions:
Here are two more ways to abuse your mark's office equipment. If you're interested in doing some serious ink damage to your mark's fax machine, just send a black piece of paper a few times (Figure 3). Another great trick is to have an <<error>> message hanging out of the fax machine or, better yet, on top of the last fax sent (Figure 4). A few other possible ideas: loading spring disengaged, spool jam, ink leaking, hair jam, and message did not send. People will wonder what the hell a loading spring is and why it's disengaged!

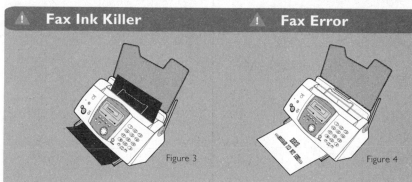

! Fax Ink Killer **! Fax Error**

Figure 3

Figure 4

BONUS

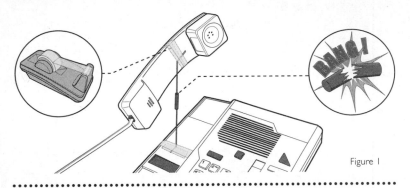

Figure 1

1) Using clear tape, fasten both ends of the string firecracker to your mark's phone.
Clear tape is a must! Once you've finished taping, place the phone back on the hook (Figure 1).

2) Call your victim's phone, or wait until he or she picks up for business.
This is your call; just be cautious when disrupting business calls from a client.

BANG!
The next time the phone rings, you'll certainly know when he or she answers it.

➡ **Who deserves this?** That guy who is constantly making personal phone calls at work.

BREAK TIME

DIFFICULTY LEVEL 1

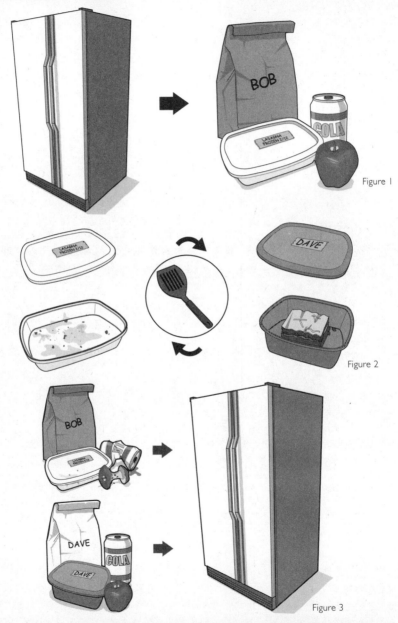

Figure 1

Figure 2

Figure 3

1) Your mission: make it appear that someone has consumed all your victim's lunch.
Of course, you could always just eat his or her lunch, which might be easier.

2) Study your victim's choice of chips, fruits, and preferred drink for a few weeks.
For example, if your victim brings a red apple every day to work, take note of it (Figure 1). This intel will help you prepare for the lunch switch when the time is right. Some of your items might come from the cafeteria, which will make your grocery shopping a whole lot easier.

3) Using a spatula, remove your victim's lunch and place it in a non-transparent airtight container.
Remove 98% of your victim's food. Using a plastic utensil tailored to your victim's dish, spread out the remaining 2% to create the illusion that someone has consumed the food. Then leave the utensil in the container, and place the container back in its original location (Figure 2).

4) Replace the full bag of chips, new fruits, and full drink with the same items, but spent.
This may be tricky, but if you did your homework, your odds will be better. Once you have replaced all the items, return everything to its original location (Figure 3).

5) Somebody has eaten all my food?
Let your coworker sob around the office for a bit, then return the original lunch.

Who deserves this? Anyone who puts his or her name on their lunch.

DIFFICULTY LEVEL I

Figure 1

Figure 2

1) Your victim's umbrella might provide protection from rain; however, it does not provide protection from you.

2) While the umbrella is collapsed, pour in your selected contents.
Glitter, Kool-Aid, and all-purpose flour work great. Carefully pour one of these ingredients into your mark's umbrella. Wipe clean any visible material (Figure 1).

3) They'll be in for a real treat the next time they step outside in the rain.
As soon as they flip the bottom spring, the canopy will open. They will realize what has happened only after the umbrella unleashes its hidden secret (Figure 2).

Who deserves this? Coworkers who are prepared for the rain, unlike you.

(!) Another suggestion:
Paper chads also work great (Figure 3). The larger the quantity, the bigger the payoff.

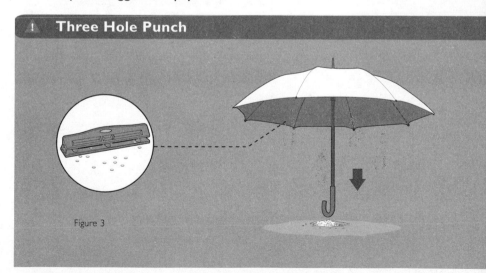

Three Hole Punch

Figure 3

DIFFICULTY LEVEL 2

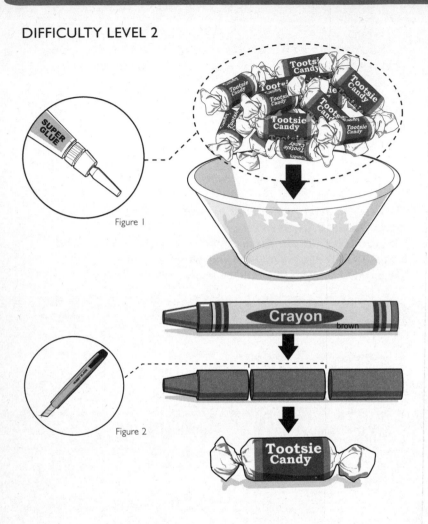

Figure 1

Figure 2

1) Purchase a small bag of desk candies.
Peppermints, root beer barrels, butterscotch—anything that comes in a small wrapping.

2) Crazy glue all the treats together and place them back into the bowl.

Glue each individualy wrapped candy together. Once finished, the candies should look as if someone had just poured free sweets into the community bowl (Figure 1).

3) Unsuspecting victims will fall prey to your sweet trap.
Place the tainted bowl of candies in a well-traveled corridor. One by one your unsuspecting victims will fall for your decoy.

4) If you don't feel like destroying a full bowl of candy, switch out one Tootsie Roll for a brown crayon.
Unwrap one of the Tootsie Roll candies and replace it with a brown crayon. Using a hobby knife, cut the brown crayon the exact length of the Tootsie Roll. Next, rough up the edges of the crayon, then roll up in the Tootsie Roll wrappings. Throw the tainted Tootsie back into the large bowl of candies (Figure 2). You can also execute this prank on someone else giving out free sweets. Walk by and make it appear as if you've taken a candy from the dish, even though you actually dropped in a Tootsie crayon.

➡ **Who deserves this?** That coworker who could really stand to lose 50 pounds.

(!) Two quick suggestions (both very naughty):
Mix up a batch of mom's favorite cookie recipe with that special laxative ingredient (Figure 3), or frost a fresh plate of Styrofoam bars complete with colorful sprinkles (Figure 4).

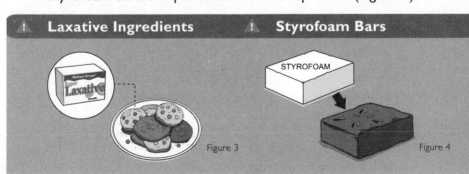

! **Laxative Ingredients**　　! **Styrofoam Bars**

STYROFOAM

Figure 3

Figure 4

DIFFICULTY LEVEL 2

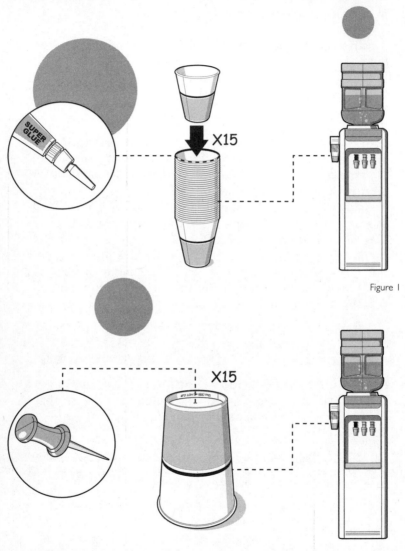

SUPER GLUE

X15

Figure 1

X15

Figure 2

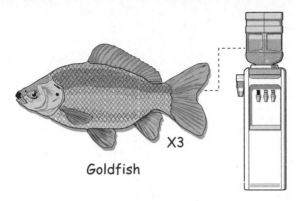

X3

Goldfish

Figure 3

....

1) A few suggestions on how to distill chaos on the watercooler.
The office watering hole is a great location to catch social butterflies with your childish antics.

- **Using adhesive, super glue the large stack of cups together.**
Now this is something to gossip about! Who the hell glued all the cups together (Figure 1)?

- **Using a pushpin, create a small hole in the bottom of the paper cup.**
Position the hole along the cup wall so it goes undetected. The number of leaky cups is solely your choice. If you decide to deface multiple cups, mix them amongst the untouched cups (Figure 2). Hey, at least you didn't poke holes on top of the jug to relieve pressure, because that would have made a huge mess.

- **A few goldfish will add life to any aquatic plastic jug.**
Purchase a few goldfish at your local pet store. Flip the water jug back over and let the fish go free. I'm not sure this is entirely sanitary, but it will probably be detected before anyone is seriously sick (Figure 3).

Who deserves this? Everyone on your last day.

DIFFICULTY LEVEL 3

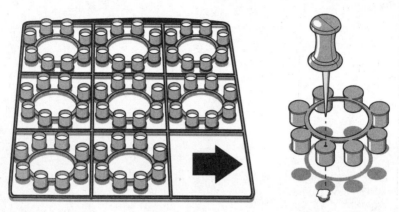

Figure 1

Figure 2

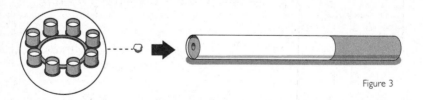

Figure 3

Figure 4

1) Purchase one package of ring caps.
These caps are designed to fit into toy guns, mostly western revolvers.

2) Remove the cap compound, using a standard pushpin.
Push the explosive compound from the back (Figure 1).

3) Acquire your mark's cigarettes, then create a hole in the end of one cigarette.
Using a pushpin again, poke a hole at the end of the cigarette that's going to be lit (Figure 2).

4) Stuff the cap explosive compound into the end of the cigarette.
I recommend using the material from only one cap. After the material is placed in the cigarette, use the pushpin to disguise the hole (Figure 3).

5) Return the cigarettes to their original location.
You can execute this on one cigarette or all cigarettes in the box—your choice (Figure 4). The next time your victim decides to take a smoke break for the sixth time that day, he or she will certainly be surprised.

 Who deserves this? The dude who goes on 6 smoke breaks a day.

DIFFICULTY LEVEL 3

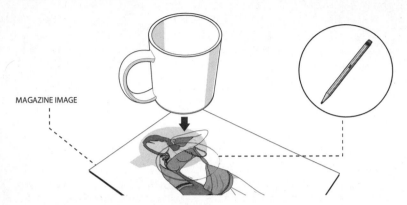

MAGAZINE IMAGE

Figure 1

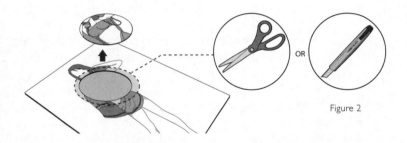

OR

Figure 2

BOTTOM OF MUG

GLUE
Multi-Purpose

Figure 3

1) Obtain your mark's coffee mug.
Best to try this before or after work hours.

2) Pick an image worth noticing.
An obscene pornographic image or a picture of you—your choice.

3) Place the mug on top of your selected image for tracing.
Using a pencil, trace the outline of your mark's coffee mug. This will help you get the exact diameter needed to cover the bottom of the mug (Figure 1).

4) Use scissors or a hobby knife to cut out the image.
The choice is yours (Figure 2).

5) Using multipurpose glue, adhere the image to the bottom of the mug.
First, apply the glue to the bottom surface of the mug. Next, place the image on top of the glue, and rub out any of the excess glue (Figure 3).

6) Return the coffee mug to the exact spot where you found it.
Your victim will casually be drinking coffee at the next team meeting and will start to notice a few eyebrows raising in his or her direction. Depending on the image, this could be very embarrassing.

Who deserves this? Anyone who talks over you at a meeting.

DIFFICULTY LEVEL 3

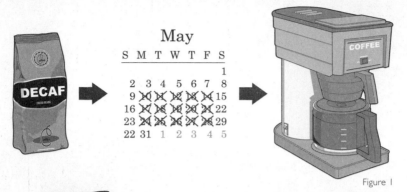

Figure 1

Figure 2

1) Put decaf in the coffee machine for 3 weeks.

You will need to switch out the current coffee first. Pour the coffee into a clean container, and save it till you have completed your experiment. Now, pour decaffeinated coffee into the original container (Figure 1). Continue to do this for approximately 3 weeks to allow everyone's system to get over caffeine withdrawal.

2) After 3 weeks, switch the decaf with espresso or a coffee high in caffeine.

Empty out the decaf coffee can into a clean container, and then pour caffeinated espresso into your empty decaf coffee can (Figure 2).

3) Notice a different mood around the office after the switch?

➡ **Who deserves this?** That caffeine junkie who paces the hallways and never actually does any work.

(!) Another suggestion:

Limit your office to 1 cup of coffee a day per individual. Using the computer, create an authentic corporate sign, and tape it onto the community coffee machine (Figure 3).

! Free Coffee Limit

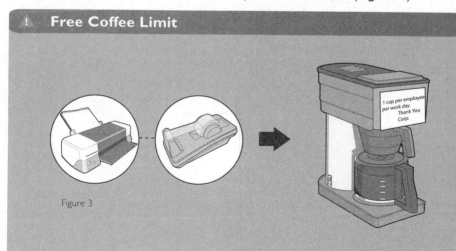

1 cup per employee per work day. Thank You Corp.

Figure 3

DIFFICULTY LEVEL 4

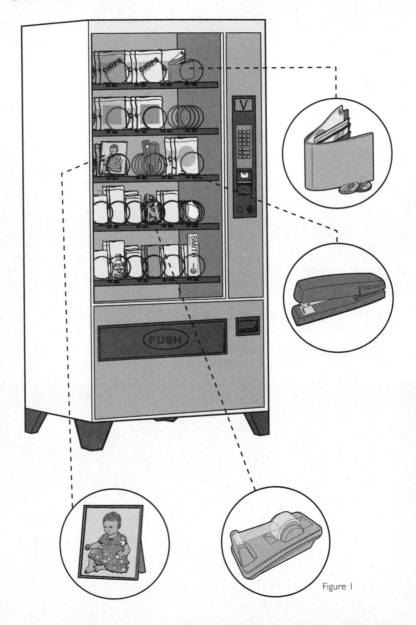

Figure 1

1) Gain access to the vending machine!
Befriend the key keeper to the vending machine.

2) Confiscate personal items from your victim's desk.
Family photos, wallet, car keys, stapler, and name tag should be at the top of your list.

3) Load the vending machine up with your victim's belongings.
Once you've gained access to the vending machine, place your victim's personal items in the merchandise slots. The only way for your mark to get her items back is to pay for them (Figure 1).

➡ **Who deserves this?** That chick who never shares her snacks.

(!) Another suggestion:
Low on cash? Tie a string around a small sponge, then stuff the sponge up the vending machine change return. You will want to make sure the sponge is out of sight and far enough up to avoid searching fingers (Figure 2). Victims will assume the change return has malfunctioned. When the time is right, pull the string and release the sponge. Consider it a bonus.

! Money Maker

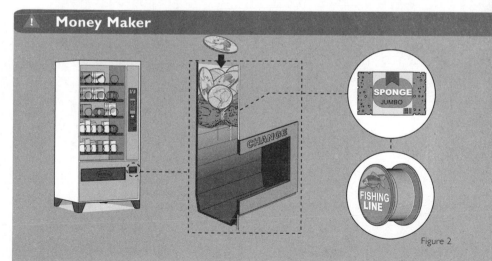

Figure 2

DIFFICULTY LEVEL 4

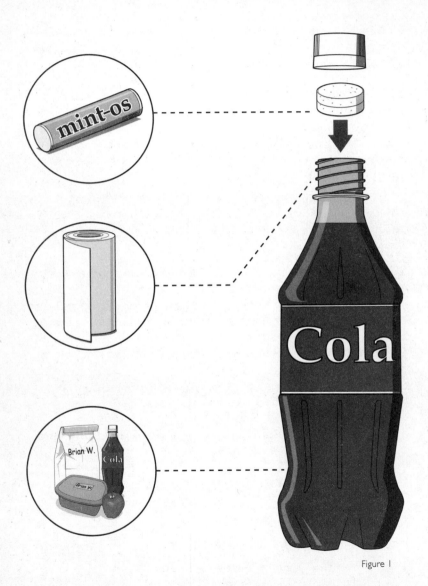

Figure 1

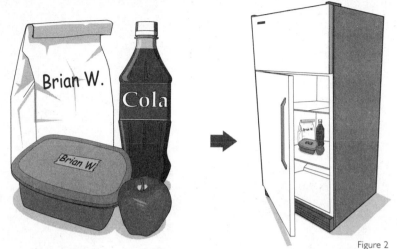

Figure 2

1) Before lunch, slip into the break room and remove your victim's cola.
This prank will work only on unopened cola products with high levels of carbonation.

2) Twist off the cap and slip one or two chewy mint candies into the bottle.
Quickly place the cap back on to the bottle to preserve as much cola as possible (Figure 1).

3) Clean the bottle surface, and remove any spilt cola
Rinse and wipe dry.

4) Return the bottle to the refrigerator.
Place the bottle back into the refrigerator by your victim's lunch (Figure 2).

5) If all goes well, your mark will unscrew the bottle, only to release a soda geyser.
The mints will create rapidly expanding carbon dioxide bubbles, which will result in a huge mess.

➡ **Who deserves this?** The pain in the ass whose lunch always smells up the entire office.

REFRIGERATOR EXPLOSION

DIFFICULTY LEVEL 4

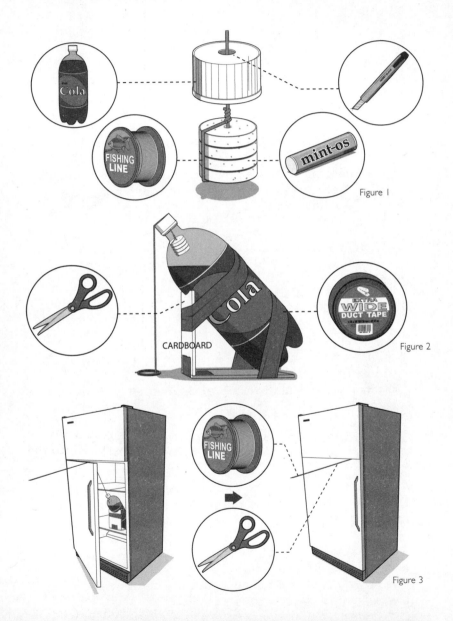

Cola

FISHING LINE

mint-os

Figure 1

CARDBOARD

EXTRA WIDE DUCT TAPE

Figure 2

FISHING LINE

Figure 3

1) Core out the center of three chewy mint candies and the center of your 2-liter cola bottle cap.
You can either drill out the centers or slowly create a hole using a pushpin (Figure 1).

2) Next, loop a line through the cap and around the candies.
Once you have passed the line through the candies, tie a knot around the three of them (Figure 1).

3) Construct a cardboard stand that will hold the cola bottle at a launch angle.
This is important. You need to design the stand so the cola bottle will geyser out of the refrigerator and not in the refrigerator (Figure 2). Use duct tape to secure the bottle onto the frame.

4) Carefully place the cap back on the bottle.
This is going to be tricky. You need to screw the cap on back the full 2-liter cola bottle without having the mints come in contact with the cola. It might work best if you tape the string to the cap, and remove the tape right before shutting the door (Figure 3).

5) While holding the string, shut the refrigerator door, then cut off any extra string.
Again, keep the mints from touching the cola while you shut the door. Once it is shut, cut off any extra string so your victim has no clue about the hidden eruption (Figure 3). As soon as your victim opens the door, the mints will fall into the bottle, creating a serious stream of cola.

Who deserves this? The guy who decides to take his lunch early.

DIFFICULTY LEVEL 5

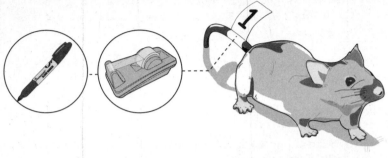

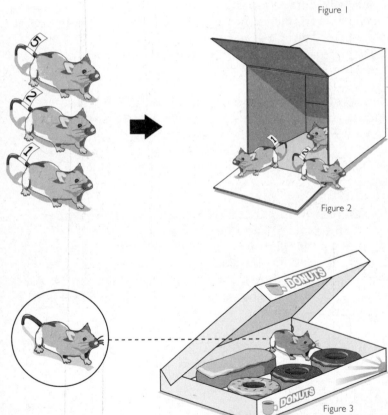

Figure 1

Figure 2

Figure 3

1) Stop by your local pet store and pick up 3 "feeder" rodents.
Some stores have decided not to sell live rodents for food, so good luck searching.

2) Label the mice 1, 2 and 5.
I recommend writing on the tape first, then looping it around the tail to make a sign (Figure 1).

3) Let the 3 mice go in the break room.
Ideally, you want a break room that will hold the mice. However, mice are great at slipping out of any space. If caught, you could lose your job and/or pay the bill for rodent removal (Figure 2).

4) 1 mouse, 2 mouse, 5 mouse?
Where are Numbers 3 and 4? That is exactly what they'll think when they round the rodents up.

➡ **Who deserves this?** The suckers who still have jobs after you have been escorted from the building.

(!) Another suggestion:
Place a fake mouse in the courtesy donut box, then close the lid and walk away (Figure 3). You will be surprised by how many people jump when they see it.

BONUS

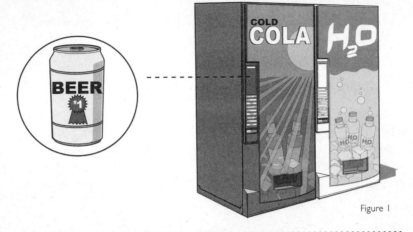

Figure 1

1) Smuggle a few cans of contraband into the office.
Perhaps being caught with alcohol at work is not a good
career choice, so conceal it.

2) Gain access to the vending machine.
It's not what you know; it's who you know. You'll need to
know where the key is kept, or who has it.

**3) Randomly place a few cans of booze in the
machine.**
A few patrons will be pleasantly surprised when they see
what came out of the machine (Figure 1).

➡ **Who deserves this?** Everyone loves the beer fairy.

LAVATORY

DIFFICULTY LEVEL 2

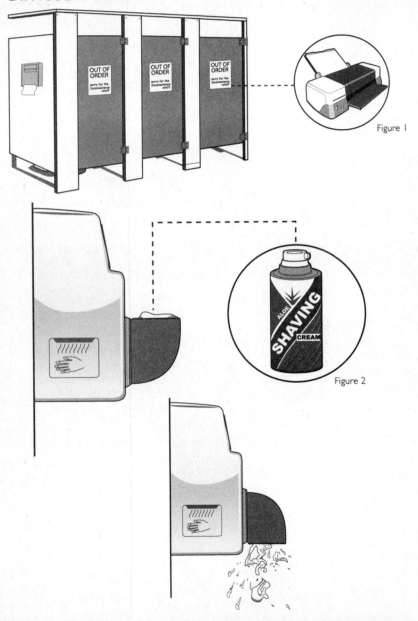

Figure 1

Figure 2

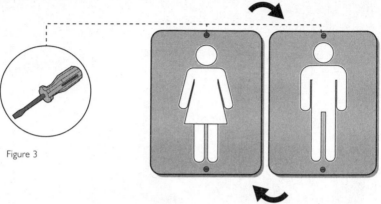

Figure 3

Having fun in the latrine.
A few cunning antics for the corporate wash room.

• **Place "Out of Order" signs on several bathroom stalls.**
Using the computer, print out authentic looking signs. If you want to bring it to the next level, "Out of Order" all the stalls (Figure 1).

• **Fill the hand dryer with shaving cream.**
Place a small amount of shaving cream in the hand dryer. Then rotate it around so it's ready for use. A small amount will probably drip out, so clean up any evidence. Then sit in one of the bathroom stalls to hear your mark's reaction (Figure 2).

• **Switch the male and female washroom signs.**
It's fairly simple but will add to a serious amount of confusion for the new guy (Figure 3).

Who deserves this? Anyone who ruins your alone time in the bathroom.

DIFFICULTY LEVEL 2

Figure 1

1) Purchase realistic artificial dog droppings.
Amazingly enough, you can find a huge selection of these on the Internet and possibly at a few party stores.

2) Bring in a few props from your own dog.
A few clumps of hair and a chewed-up ball will do nicely.

3) Place all the items on the floor in your mark's office.
Scatter the items on the floor in a small area. Once they are in place, dump a little water on the artificial dog feces for a realistic look (Figure 1).

4) If questioned by your mark about the incident, blame in on the boss's dog.
Tell your victim that you came in to work this weekend and saw the boss's dog running around the office.

➡️ **Who deserves this?** That dude who has pictures of his dog all over his cube.

(!) Another disgusting suggestion:
Not only can you purchase realistic fake dog duty, you can also purchase realistic human dung. Place one of these disgusting products on the toilet seat at work (Figure 2). If someone calls you in to investigate its authenticity, pick up with your hands to add to the amusement factor.

! Just Missed

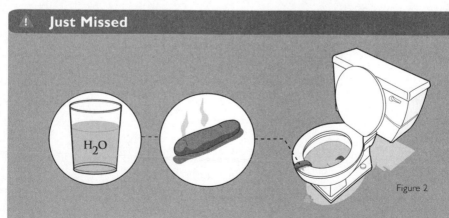

Figure 2

DIFFICULTY LEVEL 3

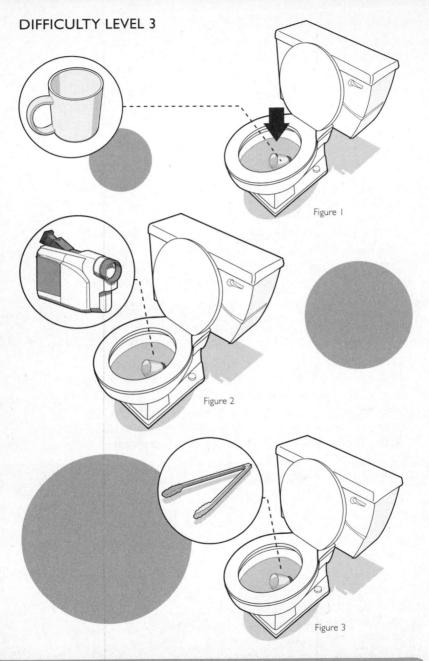

Figure 1

Figure 2

Figure 3

Figure 4

Check out this funny link...

www.youtube.com/watch?v=mugintoilet

1) Kidnap your victim's mug.
It's time for some burglarizing.

2) Place your victim's coffee mug in the toilet.
The least you can do is to make sure it's flushed before submerging the mug (Figure 1).

3) Record a short video of your accomplishment and upload the film to an Internet site.
The video should remain completely anonymous, so do not talk or film yourself in the video. Also avoid filming shoes, clothing, and your wristwatch. While recording, flush the toilet once, but make sure the mug doesn't get stuck (Figure 2)!

4) Remove the mug and return it to its original location.
Using tongs, remove the mug from the toilet (Figure 3). Next, wipe it dry and return it to your victim's desk.

5) Use the computer to create a note informing your victim of the link.
The key to this prank is to remain completely anonymous. It's best to use a computer to create the note. Place the note in front of your victim's keyboard when no one is looking. Now, from a distance, watch your victim type in the link and view your masterpiece (Figure 4).

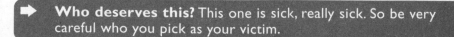

Who deserves this? This one is sick, really sick. So be very careful who you pick as your victim.

TOILET PAPER FUN

BONUS

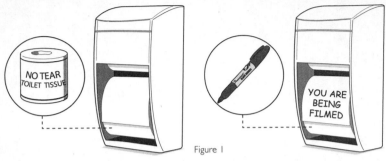

Figure 1   Figure 2

1) Purchase prank toilet paper.
You can purchase no-tear toilet tissue from the Internet.
Replace the current rolls with this irritating prank product
(Figure 1).

2) Another antic is the art of the mind game.
Using a permanent marker, leave a written message on the
toilet paper for the next user to read (Figure 2).

➡ **Who deserves this?** Someone who is daring enough to sit
on a public toilet seat.

PARKING LOT 9

DIFFICULTY LEVEL 2

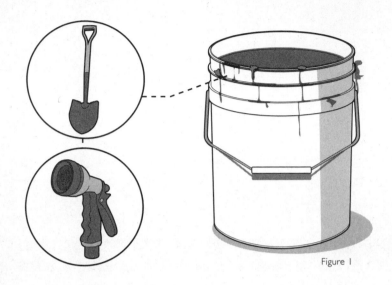

Figure 1

Figure 2

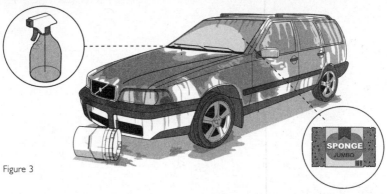

Figure 3

1) For best results, perform this dirty prank after lunch.
Your dirty work will receive maximum exposure when your victim drives out of the lot that night.

2) Mix up a semi-liquid mixture of water and soil to create gallons of mud.
Prior to driving to work, mix up several 5-gallon pails of mud (Figure 1). Avoid small stones.

3) Team up with a coworker, and begin to dump the mud all over your victim's vehicle.
Cautiously pour out the 5-gallon pails of the mud while avoiding the dirty mess yourself (Figure 2).

4) Use a sponge to create the wiper area.
This will really confuse your victim. He or she will think that you gained access to the vehicle, then drove it to an undisclosed location for some quick mud running. Clearing away the wiper area will also help your victim make it home or to the car wash safely (Figure 3). You may want to bring extra clothing, a towel, and clean water to clean your hands after you're done.

➡ Who deserves this? The guy who has the cleanest car.

DIFFICULTY LEVEL 2

Figure 1

1) Join forces with a fellow coworker.
One of your associates has decided to become a champion prankster overnight, and the lack of creativity is really starting to get to you. So, join forces with a fellow coworker and start planning this counter-strike prank.

2) Abuse the supply room.
It is important to take advantage of the company supply room as much as possible. Stock up on lots of sticky notes, or go purchase them for little more then 35 cents per 100 3 x 3 sheets . . . not bad!

3) Prepare to execute this after lunch.

After lunch, while everyone else is half asleep and using the lavatories, you both sneak out of the office and head for the parking lot. It's simple: cover every square inch of the vehicle (Figure 1). After a long day's work with a longer commute ahead, this champion prankster will walk right into a 1-hour delay.

➡️ **Who deserves this?** Anyone who has a nicer car than you.

(!) Another suggestion:

Use multiple colors to create words or obscene images (Figures 2 and 3). A few suggestions: GG2S (goody-goody two-shoes), *Brown Noser, Fired, Wash Me, Flirt, Need Raise, Working Late,* and *Payback.*

Figure 2

Figure 3

CUSTOM PLATES

DIFFICULTY LEVEL 2

Figure 1

Figure 2

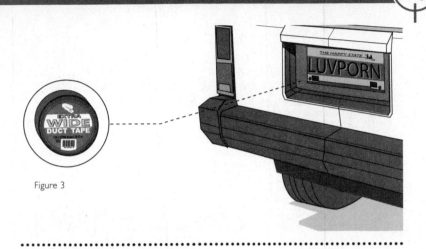

Figure 3

••

1) Recreate an authentic-looking license plate.
Using a computer, recreate the same model type as your victim's plate. You will save significant time by using a computer scanner. If you find it difficult to reconstruct the whole plate, just concentrate on the registration number (Figure 1).

2) Create a unique alphanumeric code
Decide on a slogan that best suits your victim (Figure 2).

3) Attach the new vulgar registration plate to your victim's automobile.
Using duct tape or clear packing tape, attach the new license plate. Depending on your creativity, this new custom plate should receive special attention by several passing motorists (Figure 3). He or she might not notice the plates for quite a while.

➡ Who deserves this? Anyone who has vanity license plates.

DIFFICULTY LEVEL 2

PARKING VIOLATION

Issued by Corporate Security

Date Issued	Time	Security Officer (if applicable)	Code

Location	Employee Parking Pass # (if applicable)	

Registration No. (License Plate #)	Make		State

Please accept this warning in a professional manner, this violation citation will <u>not</u> be disputed.

☐ **UNNECESSARY SPEEDS IN LOT**

☐ **POLLUTION (NOISE/TRASH)**

☐ _____

STRIKE

1 **2** **3**

tear off

office Use only
741384

Corporate Security has implemented a new system to insure the safety of our employees and visitors as well as its facilities and property. This new system is based off of the **Three Strike Rule**. Once any one vehicle is issued three **PARKING VIOLATIONS,** that vehicle could be subject to a towing and possible criminal action.

Figure 1

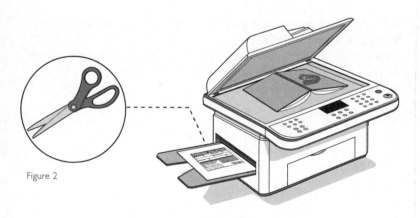

Figure 2

Figure 3

1) 1 week prior to executing this prank, plant the seed.
Tell your victim that you noticed security writing a ticket in the corporate lot.

2) Use a photocopier to reproduce this parking violation, or purchase fake tickets on the Internet.
After copying, cut on the dotted line (Figures 1 and 2).

3) Fill out your victim's vehicle information on the bogus parking violation.
To make it look authentic, fill it out quickly. Mark down the reason for the citation, then place it under your victim's wiper blade (Figure 3).

4) A victim who is gullible to believe the first one will probably believe the second one as well.
Ask your victim if he was driving too fast in the parking lot to deserve a ticket. If the answer is yes, he will start to assume he really is guilty.

Who deserves this? The guy who's already had a few citations this year.

DIFFICULTY LEVEL 2

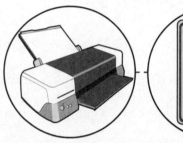

Figure 1

Figure 2

Figure 3

1) There is a large variety of parking signs in your lot that can be customized.
Using the computer, this will only take minutes.

2) Visitor Parking only!
What kind of visitors? Left-handed people, blind people, divorced people, or porn stars (Figure 1).

3) No parking at any time!
Just switch out the word "Parking" (Figure 2). If you hate your job, use expletives.

(!) Another suggestion:
Exit signs can also be easily manipulated for humorous sayings and informational purposes (Figure 3). It's good to know that the bar and the weekend are just out that door.

➡ **Who deserves this?** The coworker who wouldn't let you in his car pool.

DIFFICULTY LEVEL 2

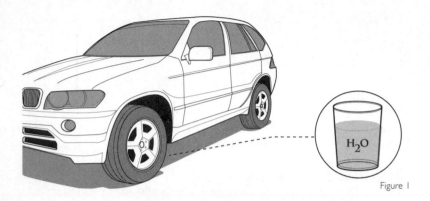

Figure 1

Figure 2

1) Fancy new car!

Usually after bonus time, a few new cars start to show up in the company lot.

2) Pour a huge glass of water under the engine compartment.

When pouring out the water, make sure that it's visible from the driver's door, so your victim notices the mysterious leak when he or she approaches their car. Also, it is very important to pour out the water toward the end of the day, so the water doesn't evaporate (Figure 1).

3) What the hell?

Your victim will see it and immediately assume a mechanical problem (Figure 2).

4) Regularly pull this off until your victim decides it's time for service.

However, stop him right before he calls for a check-up.

➡ **Who deserves this?** Any coworker who obviously got a bonus big enough to buy a new car.

(!) Another suggestion:

First off, do not pour sugar in your victim's gas tank. Instead, put an empty sugar container next to your victim's gas tank, and sprinkle some sugar around on the ground (Figure 3). He or she will see it and fear the worst!

! Sugar Tank Stage

Figure 3

DIFFICULTY LEVEL 3

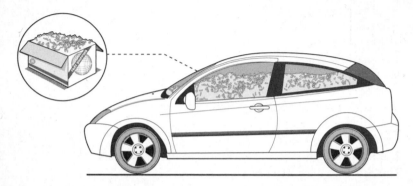

Figure 1

Figure 2

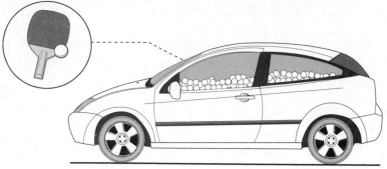

Figure 3

1) Fill it up please!
The key to revenge is getting the key of your victim's car.

- **By utilizing the sunroof, pour in packing peanuts.**
  This stuffing is probably the best material for your buck. Foam plastic peanuts are dirt cheap and come in huge bulk packages. They are available in your mailroom and in office supply stores (Figure 1).

- **Paper shreds are virtually impossible to clean up.**
  With huge bags of paper shreds sitting by the back door of your company, it would be a shame not to reuse them one last time before they are processed into new paper. Paper shreds are quite easy to pack into a car; however, it is unpacking them that is a pain in the ass (Figure 2).

- **Sports balls.**
  Used tennis balls, golf range balls, kick balls, and Ping-Pong balls are good items (Figure 3). You can purchase used bulk lots on the Internet.

➡ **Who deserves this?** The guy who never offers to drive during lunch.

DIFFICULTY LEVEL 3

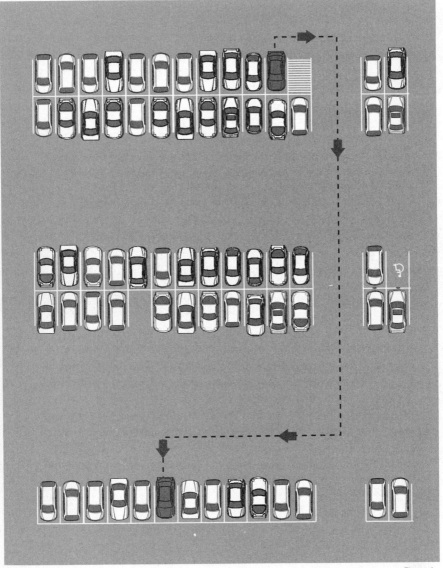

Figure 1

1) Acquire the keys to a coworker's automobile.
Swipe the keys when no one is looking. Men often place their keys next to their computer so they don't have to walk around all day with the keys filling their pockets.

2) Run out after lunch and locate the vehicle.
Once you've found it, move it to a new location, like the back corner of the lot (Figure 1).

3) Return keys to their original location.
Lock the doors and return the keys to their original location. Your mark will walk around aimlessly, wondering where the heck he or she parked this morning. Do this several times over a month.

4) Don't forget to turn up the sound!
When you're in the car, jack up the radio before turning off the car.

➡ **Who deserves this?** The guy who leaves his keys on his desk.

(!) Another suggestion:
Put your victim's keys in a shallow cup of water, then place the cup and keys in the freezer (Figure 2). Depending on the freezer's setting, the keys may be frozen by the time work is finished up. You can leave a note telling your victim of the location of his keys, or just return the frozen cup to him.

! Frozen Key

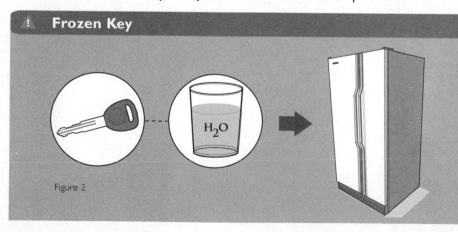

H_2O

Figure 2

DIFFICULTY LEVEL 2

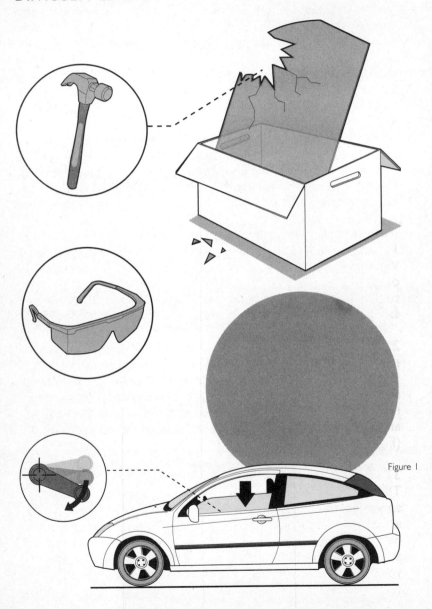

Figure 1

Figure 2

1) **You'll need a small piece of automotive glass.**
When automotive glass shatters, it breaks into thousands of small pieces to reduce injury. Stop by a local glass shop to see if you can get a small amount of waste for free. Wear safety glasses if attempting to break glass yourself (Figure 1).

2) **Roll down the window to give the illusion that it's missing.**
Gain access to your friend's car, and roll down the window (Figure 2). Begin to spread the broken glass around to recreate a break-in. Place a small amount on the pavement and seat, and most of it on the floor mats for easy clean-up (Figure 3).

3) **Time to call your local glass specialist.**
There is a really good chance your victim will call a glass specialist and make an appointment. Who's going to roll up a window that appears broken? It should be interesting to hear the reaction when your victim brings the car in and still has a perfectly good window in the door. Just make sure your victim doesn't receive a bill for replacing a window.

 Who deserves this? Messing with a dude's car is grounds for an ass-kicking, so make sure this is someone you could beat up.

PARALLEL PARK

DIFFICULTY LEVEL 5

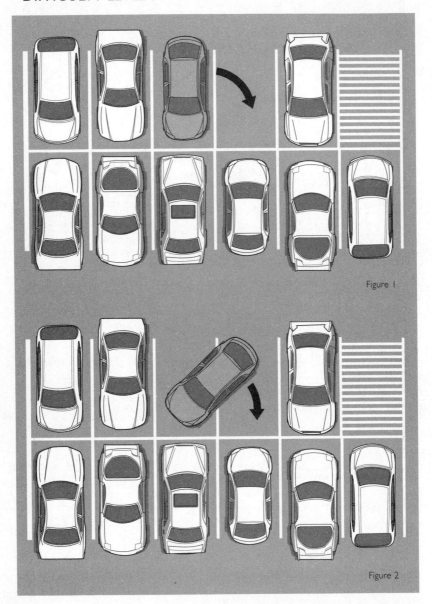

Figure 1

Figure 2

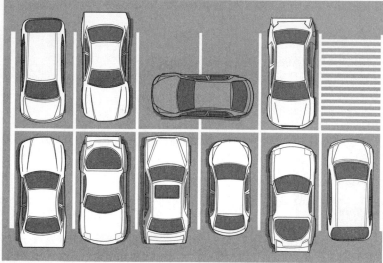

Figure 2

1) This prank is designed for lightweight compact cars and 6 to 10 guys.
Believe it or not, it's possible to pick up a small car.

2) It is important to do small short lifts in order to avoid injury.
With a team of guys, start at the back and slowly rotate the vehicle into the adjacent parking spot (Figure 1).

3) It will take several lifts to move it into place.
Once you've started to position the car, you may have to move to the front and do a few lifts (Figure 2).

4) Fits like a glove!
Your victim will have to wait until everyone has left the building before he or she can drive out (Figure 3).

Who deserves this? This is a great team prank to play on that prick who pisses everyone off.